EINSTEIN'S BEACH HOUSE

STORIES

JACOB M. APPEL

PRESSGANG

2014

PRESSGANG

4600 Sunset Avenue
Indianapolis, IN 46208
pressgang.butler.edu

These stories have appeared in the following journals and anthologies:

"Hue and Cry" in *Gettysburg Review*; "La Tristesse Des Hérissons" in *Tusculum Review*; "Strings" in *Chariton Review*; "Limerence" as "Marston Moor" in *Pleiades*; "Einstein's Beach House" in *Sonora Review*; "The Rod of Asclepius" in *The New Guard*; "Sharing the Hostage" in *The Wisconsin Review*; and "Paracosmos" in *Nimrod*.

Published 2014 by Pressgang
Book Design by Zachary Roth and the Butler Pub Lab.
Set in Crimson Text; titling in League Gothic and LSTK Bembo.
"Tentacle sketch" copyright © 2012 by Mark Fairless
darkusmarkus.prosite.com

First edition October 2014

ISBN: 978-0-9849405-8-5
Library of Congress Control Number: 2014942699

Manufactured in the United States of America

PRAISE FOR JACOB M. APPEL

"Appel's stories move with thirstful purpose, rarely slowing, filled with wry humor and *bon mots* as we proceed briskly down his fictional paths, invited to examine modern ethical issues along the way."

—Matthew Pitt, author of *Attention Please Now*

"Impossibly keen . . . a collection that takes a sharp look at the moments when we, whether child or adult, see who we truly are, and the inevitability of who we will become. Appel's achy, skewed, sometimes heart-breaky world is dense with truth and humor—the stuff of great literature."

—Allison Lynn, author of *The Exiles* and *Now You See It*

"Lives are coming apart, and coming together, in stories that live with you long after you've read them. Comparisons to Cheever, Trevor, and especially Chekhov can't be helped, but Appel writes with a grace and humor all his own."

—Dan O'Brien, author of *War Reporter* and
The Body of an American

"Appel approaches his characters with compassion and an understanding of human frailty."

—*Kirkus Review*

"The dialog, even when one of the speakers wobbles on the verge of madness, shows bite and intelligence . . . The rambunctious serendipity recalls T.C. Boyle, as does the ability to turn on a dime, now cutthroat, now huggable."

—John Domini, *The Brooklyn Rail*

"Appel captures the sounds, smells and feeling of human idiosyncrasies, describing each person and place with layers of specifics and closely observed characters."

—Anne M. Drolet, *North American Review*

For Rosalie

CONTENTS

EINSTEIN'S BEACH HOUSE

HUE AND CRY

THAT YEAR LIZZIE'S KID SISTER kept a list of things that were funny when they happened to other people: tarring and feathering, Peeping Toms, mad cow disease. The rare encephalopathy from which their father suffered didn't actually come from eating infected cattle, it turned out, but from a spontaneous somatic mutation—what Bill Sucram's neurologist described as "losing the genetic lottery"—yet the ailment was enough like mad cow that Lizzie's mother swore off animal products. Overnight, Myra Sucram stopped fricasseeing duck and took to ordering exotic soy dishes from a newly opened kosher-vegan deli on Walloon Street. Her family's health consumed her: she spent mornings arguing with Bill's insurance carrier, afternoons researching manganese contamination and do-it-yourself dioxin tests at the public library, and evenings promising her husband and daughters that medical breakthroughs can happen overnight. She wore her smile like a shroud.

Lizzie's father resigned himself to his diagnosis. He informed the Pontefract Board of Education that he had six months to live and that he did not intend to spend them at the office. Then he composed a list of people who harbored him ill will—a shady plumber he'd sued in small-claims court, his estranged stepbrother in Las Vegas—and he telephoned each one to apologize. One night, the thirty-eight-year-old agnostic middle school principal summoned his daughters to hot cocoa at the kitchen table and announced: "I fear I've taught you girls too much grammar and not enough forgiveness." So Lizzie was mortified, yet not unprepared, when their father insisted on taking them to meet the sex offender.

The sex offender's name was Rex Benbow. He'd been staying inside his grandmother's modest bungalow at the end of their block for nearly two weeks, the subject of protests and countless flyers, but Lizzie had been far too concerned with her father's wellbeing and her own hopeless crush on her best friend, Julia Sand, to give the parolee a second thought—until Julia confessed to a fascination with the man. Suddenly, he acquired the allure of an outlaw.

"My brother has been spying on the place. He says the cops aren't protecting his house anymore," said Julia. "So the coast is clear."

"Clear for what?"

"Clear for us."

The girls sat side by side on the swing set on the playground of their former elementary school. At thirteen, their long legs now reached the muddy earth below—Lizzie in acid-wash jeans, Julia in a denim skirt over tights. The pair had been meeting after school like this all autumn, a coven of two, sometimes sipping liqueurs in miniature bottles pinched from Dr. Sand's study. Today, they were sober. It was the first week since the clocks had fallen back, and slender shadows darkened the nearby playing fields.

"Have you gone totally crazy?" demanded Lizzie. "You don't really plan on trying to meet him, do you?"

"Meet him? Who said anything about meeting him?" Julia laughed playfully. Her green eyes turned all feline. "We're not going to find out anything interesting by meeting him. What we need to do is wait until he goes out—I mean, the guy has to come out eventually—and then we'll sneak inside to explore."

That was the audacity that rendered Julia so alluring, the same leap-and-then-look mindset that would get her hooked on heroin three years later. The intensity stamped on the girl's delicate features frightened Lizzie—but she found this danger magnetic, disarming. It mattered nothing to Julia that her own father and older brother were among the "concerned citizens" going door to door with petitions aimed at driving the sex offender from the neighborhood.

Julia added that, according to her brother, Alice Benbow, crippled by age and disappointment and a progressive lung ailment, no longer left her first-floor bedroom. So as long as they kept quiet, they'd have free roam of the house.

"You're not afraid, are you?" Julia asked.

Lizzie gnawed on the string of her sweatshirt hood. Headlights panned the playing field as a station wagon made a U-turn in the elementary school parking lot. "I just don't get what you're expecting to find," said Lizzie. "Do you really think he's going to leave stuff lying around?"

"You are afraid," snapped Julia.

"Okay, I'm afraid. Why shouldn't I be afraid?" Lizzie lowered her voice. "I've got enough stress without worrying about getting raped and murdered."

Julia laughed again. "Nobody is going to get raped and murdered," she said, accentuating Lizzie's concerns so they sounded foolish. "At least, we won't. Not if we're prepared." She reached into her purse and withdrew a double-edged boot knife. Lizzie instinctively raised her hand to her throat.

"See, we're fine," said Julia. "Besides, he likes boys."

Lizzie's veranda offered an unobstructed view of Alice Benbow's bungalow, so the girls ensconced themselves on the porch and waited. Although Bill and Myra Sucram weren't the type to suspect mischief, Julia insisted that they set up a pair of easels and paint the autumn foliage, just in case their constant presence on the terrace drew notice. To Lizzie, this seemed like overkill—yet she dutifully filled her canvas with bright hues of amber and vermillion. Meanwhile, her partner brazenly painted the Benbow dwelling itself: a flawless facsimile, down to the stars on the tattered curbside flag and the tire treads on Alice's rusting wheelbarrow.

Their first week of espionage proved a washout: nobody entered or left the Benbow house for five straight evenings. Of course, it was possible that Rex conducted his excursions in the mornings while the girls were at school, but Lizzie didn't have the courage to suggest this to Julia. Most days, they had the porch entirely to themselves, except for the occasions when Lizzie's eleven-year-old sister, Rebecca, an aspiring newspaper reporter, asked them to use vocabulary words for her in context: vertiginous, mandrake, cantilever. Also vigilante, pedophile. Once, as twilight approached, Myra served them hot chocolate and then sat silently in a wicker chair while they drank—looking as though she wanted to share something profound. Several times, Bill Sucram steered his motorized wheelchair down the makeshift plank that covered the porch steps and complimented the girls on their artistic efforts. "Few hobbies more wholesome than painting," he said. "And if you two ever want a live model," he added, winking, "you just ask." At those moments, Lizzie felt a twinge of remorse that she wasn't spending more time with her father—and less with Julia—but then she'd hear her friend's electrifying voice, and the guilt would pass.

Julia's precautions did ultimately prove prescient, but not as protection against the suspicions of the Sucrams. Rather, it was her own father and brother who appeared on Lizzie's porch that Saturday morning, the latter armed with a clipboard. Dr. Sand and his son had lantern jaws and deep-set black eyes; in their matching cardigan sweaters, they reminded Lizzie of Mormon missionaries. Julia herself referred to her family as "victims of the body snatchers" and often claimed she was a changeling.

"Fancy meeting you here, Julia," said Dr. Sand as though this were the world's funniest quip. "Morning, Elizabeth. Your parents home?"

Lizzie leaned through the front door and shouted for her father. Less than a minute passed before Bill Sucram emerged from the house.

"Morning, Bill," said Dr. Sand. "How are you holding up?"

"Not too bad for a man with Swiss cheese for brains," said Lizzie's father. "But keep an eye on me. Yesterday I tried to unlock my car door with my toothbrush."

Dr. Sand smiled uncomfortably. His son stood at broad-shouldered attention, the clipboard behind his back. Julia continued to paint.

"I'm joking," said Bill. "Cut me some slack. I have to cram thirty years of bad humor into six months."

"Of course," agreed Dr. Sand. "In any case, my boy and I are trying to persuade the town to enact an ordinance prohibiting sex offenders from residing within five hundred yards of children under eighteen."

"Are you now?" inquired Lizzie's father.

"We're hoping you'd be willing to sign. Your wife, too, if she's around."

Julia's older brother stepped forward with the clipboard.

"And why exactly do we need such a law?" asked Bill.

Dr. Sand glanced at the girls, then up the block toward the Benbow house.

"I thought you'd be more aware of what's going on. I don't want to delve into details at the moment," he said, looking pointedly at Lizzie and Julia, "but there's a level-one predator living on your block. Haven't you seen our flyers?"

"Oh, I've seen your flyers," said Lizzie's father. "But as far as I'm concerned, punishment is the job of the criminal justice system. I'm in the business of forgiving people, not harassing them."

Dr. Sand's face lost its color, but his voice remained level. "I don't think that's an accurate characterization, Bill. We're not harassing anyone . . . You're an educator. And a father. Surely you must . . ."

"Must I? Well, I don't," said Bill. "In fact, I've been thinking of inviting the poor fellow over for dinner."

That was too much for Dr. Sand. "I won't pretend to understand, Mr. Sucram," he said, shaking his head like a preacher befuddled by sin. He turned so quickly that he nearly toppled his son. Lenny Sand flashed his sister a look of warning on his own retreat down the steps.

"When holes start sprouting inside your brain," Sucram called after them, "you may see things differently."

Lizzie watched the Sands knock on the neighbor's door. The dentist presented his petition to elderly Mrs. Greenbough, who kept asking Dr. Sand to speak louder until the dentist was forced to shout his proposed ordinance into the tranquility of the suburban morning. Then Sucram apologized to the girls for disrupting their work and wheeled himself back inside the house.

"Your dad is awesome," said Julia. "Totally awesome."

⚜

Another three days elapsed without any signs of life at the corner bungalow—and then, on Tuesday afternoon, the girls returned home from school to find the Benbows' garage door rolled up. As they watched, dumbstruck, a twenty-year-old Lincoln Town Car, glistening with tail fins and suicide doors, eased into the driveway; the driver exited the vehicle and pulled the garage door shut behind him. When the car passed Lizzie's porch, the girls recognized Rex Benbow—older, but unmistakably the face from the flyers—at the helm. Instantly perspiration erupted on Lizzie's neck and along the bellies of her forearms.

"Okay, babe, it's now or never," declared Julia. "Tell your mom we're walking downtown to see a movie."

Lizzie did as instructed. Then she trailed Julia up the block and around the corner onto Fleming Street—where they advanced ten meters before backtracking into the Benbows' rear yard. Julia plucked two pocket flashlights from her purse, tested each inside her cupped palm, and handed one to Lizzie. "I did some reconnaissance last week," Julia whispered, and, to Lizzie's amazement, her friend retrieved a crowbar from behind the septic tank. Seconds later, she had pried open a cellar window and vanished into the darkness below. By the time Lizzie built up the courage to follow—or rather, by the time the terror of entering had paled compared to the fear of disappointing her closest friend—Julia had already switched on the overhead light.

The finished basement smelled of mildew. Watermarks from remote floods scarred the linoleum. Along one wall, built-in shelves contained cartons marked GLASSWARE, and board games, and a haphazard assortment of books. More books covered a warped Ping-Pong table. In the far corner, a pair of stilts leaned against a sofa missing several cushions. A side door opened onto a small vestibule that contained a washer and dryer, and another door led to a windowless bathroom. What struck Lizzie was how ordinary the room appeared: her own basement would likely look the same in two more decades when she was the sex offender's age, except that her father had invested in a table for billiards instead of Ping-Pong. She wondered whether she and Julia would still be friends then—or more than friends—and whether they would reminisce about the crazy evening when they sneaked into the sex offender's basement.

"What are we looking for?" Lizzie asked.

"I don't know yet," hissed Julia. "We'll know it when we find it."

Julia honed in on a metal filing cabinet opposite the bathroom. Lizzie watched over her friend's shoulder as the girl rummaged through folders of Alice Benbow's tax returns and medical bills from her late daughter's chemotherapy. Eventually, Lizzie's attention drifted to the volumes on the shelves: Xenophon's *Anabasis*, CliffsNotes to *Jude the Obscure*, *Peterson's A Field Guide to the Birds of Virginia*. Nothing pornographic, nothing more risqué than the collected works of D. H. Lawrence.

"Nothing down here," said Julia. "Let's go."

She grabbed Lizzie by the hand and led her up the basement stairs to the first floor of the bungalow. Sweat mixed with sweat in their palms. They tiptoed across the tiled kitchen and into the narrow foyer, where the hardwood floorboards whimpered under their feet. A door stood ajar along the corridor, revealing the flicker and din of the nightly news. They edged past the grandmother's room, one at a time, like pioneers traversing a rickety bridge. And suddenly, after they'd both slid by safely, an ancient voice cried out, "Rex? Are you home already?"

Julia reached for Lizzie's hand again and squeezed. Lizzie didn't dare to exhale. From Alice Benbow's room rose the flat, soothing voice of Tom Brokaw announcing the formal dissolution of Czechoslovakia. The grandfather clock in the foyer ticked away the seconds, but Lizzie lost track of time. When the old woman had remained silent for what must have been five minutes—but felt like several generations—Julia tugged on Lizzie's arm and steered her into the sex offender's bedroom.

The girls navigated the chamber by flashlight. A matching rosewood chiffonier and bowfront dresser stood on either side of the window; additional drawers ran beneath the platform bed. Vintage movie posters covered the interior walls: *Paper Moon, The Man Who Would Be King.* On the nightstand rested a pair of reading glasses, a Bible, and an ashtray full of cigarette stubs. Julia ran her hand under the carefully folded bedcovers, under the pillow and mattress, behind the dresser. She found nothing salacious or remotely incriminating. She yanked open the drawers below the bed and discovered collections of stamps and baseball cards. Lizzie perched atop the edge of the bedspread and thought to herself: I'm in a sex offender's bedroom. I'm sitting on a sex offender's bed. She turned off her flashlight. At some point, Julia climbed up beside her on the bed.

"I'm sure there's something here," whispered Julia. "We just don't know where to look. Think, Lizzie: if you were a pervert, where would you hide stuff?"

"I don't know. I guess if it was that important, I'd take it with me."

Lizzie hadn't meant her words to sound like a challenge, but in the darkened room they came across as more aggressive than she'd intended. Her head was swimming. She wished she could spend eternity alone like this with Julia, yet part of her brain was warning her to flee immediately.

"You're right. You're right, and I'm an idiot! Of course, he's taken it with him," declared Julia. "Dammit, Lizzie. Why do you have to be so brilliant?"

Lizzie waited for Julia to say more, but she didn't. She sensed her friend alongside her on the sex offender's bed, the warmth of Julia's breath branding her neck, and she sensed some subtle, inchoate shift occurring between them. She did not dare to move or speak. And then, with no warning, the door opened and Lizzie found herself blinded by the overhead light. As her eyes adjusted, the form of Rex Benbow appeared across the room. He sported a plaid hunting cap and had a knapsack draped over one shoulder. Lizzie was afraid to glance at Julia—afraid that her friend might draw her knife.

"You girls should go home," said Rex Benbow. The sex offender didn't sound angry, just fatigued. "I don't want any trouble."

"We saw the front door open," said Julia, her tone calm and composed. "You really shouldn't leave your door open like that."

"Please," said Benbow. "You can't be here."

Lizzie waited for Julia's next move. The sounds of the television drifted down the corridor, punctuated suddenly by the old woman's voice: "What's going on, Rex? Is someone with you?"

"Nothing, Grandma," called out Benbow. "Only the radio."

He stepped away from the doorframe and looked desperately at the girls. Julia stood up. "I think we've overstayed our welcome, Lizzie," she said, and then she led Lizzie into the foyer and down the Benbows' front steps. Overhead, a low ceiling of clouds kept the night cool and damp. The girls retreated to Lizzie's porch without speaking, and, in the sharp autumn air, Lizzie found herself wondering whether the sensation she'd felt on the bed—the tingle that something had shifted—was real or imagined.

"What are you thinking?" Julia finally asked.

Lizzie didn't dare answer honestly. "I'm glad you didn't stab him," she said.

Chagrin spread across Julia's features, but Lizzie was never certain whether Julia had been disappointed with her response or with the evening as a whole.

"Did you see that knapsack?" Julia demanded. "You were so right about him taking things with him. Next time we'll sneak in while he's at home—maybe when he's sleeping."

After breakfast the following Saturday, Bill Sucram took his daughters to meet the sex offender. Lizzie had listened to her parents argue about Bill's idea into the early hours of the morning—her ear plastered to the wall separating her bedroom from theirs—and at one point her mother snapped, "Fuck forgiveness! They should cut his cock off," but by the time Myra Sucram summoned her daughters downstairs for vegan French toast and strips of soy bacon, she had acquiesced to the inevitable. "Your father has an outing planned for you girls," she said with apparent cheer, as though her husband were taking her daughters apple picking or Christmas shopping. Myra's soft, beleaguered face betrayed no hint of her prior anger. "I do hope you don't already have plans, Lizzie."

Lizzie had in fact promised her entire day to Julia. Her friend had found a tattoo artist in Richmond who didn't check IDs. Yet as much as it pained Lizzie to bail on her—the girls hadn't spent meaningful time together since their encounter with Rex Benbow—her father's increasing frailty left her no real choice. Lizzie was a good girl, at heart, and she did not wish to disappoint him.

Bill insisted that his daughters spruce up for the occasion. Lizzie squeezed into the somber ankle-length skirt she'd worn to her grandmother's funeral, while Rebecca wore a checkered gingham dress with a baby blue sash that reminded Lizzie of the Judy Garland impersonators at the Easter parade. "You two look fit for an audience with the queen," declared Bill, his voice already dysarthric from disease. "Okay, we're off," he added, as he wheeled himself onto the front porch. "We'll be back home for lunch."

"And if you're not?" Myra asked.

Lizzie's father let the question evaporate into the air. He navigated his motorized wheelchair onto the asphalt and then jolted his way up the Benbows' slate path. His daughters followed. Dead leaves of various hues coated the Benbow yard. Two doors away, Mrs. Greenbough's Irish setter stood alert at the perimeter of an invisible fence, yapping at a birdbath beyond her reach. Lizzie suffered under the grasp of her pantyhose, which made her feel like an old woman.

Rebecca pressed the doorbell.

A long silence yielded to footsteps, but the door did not open. Rebecca looked at her father for guidance, and he signaled for her to ring the bell again. Once more, a long silence ensued. Lizzie was already marshalling the courage to suggest that they return home when a voice from within said, "Please, go away." Instantly Lizzie recognized Rex Benbow's flat inflection, and she nearly lost control of her bladder. "My grandmother is old and sick," added Benbow. "We don't want any trouble."

"We're not here to make trouble," replied Bill. "I'm your neighbor, Bill Sucram. My daughters and I wanted to welcome you to the block. That's all."

They waited. From behind the door, they heard the sound of Benbow's voice—but muffled and distant, likely addressed to his grandmother.

"I'm not leaving until you shake my hand," called Lizzie's father. "Let us show our good will, and we'll go home."

Lizzie bargained mutely with a god she didn't actually believe in, offering up all aspects of model citizenship if the sex offender didn't open the door. "He wants to be left alone, Dad," she argued. "Please. You can't force yourself on him." Yet a second later, Lizzie's prayers were answered by a chorus of multiple dead bolts unlocking.

Rex Benbow stood in the doorway, wearing the same plaid hunting cap. His arms hung limp and simian at his sides. Lizzie's father introduced himself for the second time and extended his hand to the sex offender. Rex shook it tentatively.

"These are my daughters," said Lizzie's dad. "Elizabeth and Rebecca."

Lizzie waited for Rex to recognize her. She contemplated denying his accusations: It would be her word against his, a teenager against a convicted predator. In the nearby hedge, chickadees and titmice cavorted innocently. Lizzie felt the sex offender's gaze on her, but she dared not meet it.

"Glad to meet you both," said Rex.

Rebecca volunteered her hand to the sex offender. Lizzie felt obliged to offer hers as well. The man's grip was lifeless, but his dull eyes met hers and sealed their secret. Lizzie suddenly understood that Benbow feared her more than she feared him—and that this daytime visit caused him far more pain than had their nighttime intrusion.

"May we come in?" asked Sucram.

The sex offender hesitated for a moment and then opened the door fully, allowing Lizzie's father to wheel into the foyer. "You'll forgive me for not having anything to offer you," said Rex. "We don't get many visitors."

Rex Benbow led them down the same corridor that Lizzie had explored with Julia earlier that week, taking them into a tidy, dimly lit sitting room. The furnishings, sturdy and utilitarian, recalled the 1950s. A bricked-up fireplace defined one of the walls, and near the heavily shaded bay windows three tall stools surrounded a coaster bar. The upholstery reeked of stale tobacco. Not only did the place appear ordinary, Lizzie noted, but it also looked rather shabby.

At the sex offender's behest, the girls seated themselves around the coffee table. Sucram drew up his chair alongside their host's. And then the interruption of the previous evening replayed itself.

"Who's there?" cried Alice Benbow.

"It's all right, Grandma," Rex called out. "It's just the neighbors." He turned to them and added, apologetically, "She won't remember in ten minutes."

How different Lizzie felt about the grandmother now: in the light of day, she pitied the unfortunate woman imprisoned with her exiled offspring. She almost felt sorry for the sex offender himself. Rex was sitting with his hands folded in his lap, jaw clenched, clearly waiting for the visit to end—but Sucram seemed utterly oblivious to the poor man's discomfort.

"What I came over here to say," Lizzie's father was saying, "is that I know everyone in Pontefract hasn't been entirely welcoming to you, but I don't want you to think that those elements represent the entire community. Or even the majority. As far as I'm concerned, people have a right to atone for their mistakes. You've served your time. Whatever you've done in the past is now between you and your conscience."

"Thank you," said Rex.

Lizzie longed for her father to stop—to leave the poor man to his private misery—but she didn't dare intervene. It struck her that her father and the sex offender were roughly the same age, that they were both relatively young and futureless. Rebecca had slipped a small notepad out of her pocket and was scribbling away ferociously like a cub journalist.

"We should have you over for dinner one night," said Bill. "I'm sure my wife would love to meet you—and it might be good for you to get out of the house."

Rex stared at his own hands. "I wouldn't want to

impose . . ."

"Nonsense. It would be our pleasure," said Lizzie's father. "We'll have to do it sooner rather than later, though, because it turns out I'm dying. Holes in the brain. Like a giant sponge. But it's not contagious—not unless I donate a cornea to you, at least—so there's nothing to worry about."

"I don't like to leave my grandmother alone," said Rex.

"That's very conscientious of you," answered Bill. "But we could find a way to work around that. Maybe one of the girls could stay with her . . ."

"I don't like to leave my grandmother," Rex said again, but now his voice sounded more desperate, like a man losing his grip on a ledge.

"You'll think it over, Mr. Benbow, won't you?" interjected Lizzie. "When you do decide you're ready to have dinner, you'll give us a call." She had no idea where the words arose from—and they shocked her as much as they did her host. Even Rebecca stopped scribbling and glanced up in surprise.

Rex flashed Lizzie a look of relief and gratitude. "Yes, I'll do that."

Lizzie stood up, and Rex did the same. It was almost as if they had choreographed their interaction in advance. As the pair inched toward the corridor, Sucram finally sensed that their visit was drawing to a close. "I hope you will call," he urged. "You have nothing to be ashamed of— at least as far as we're concerned." Rex Benbow thanked Lizzie's father once again as he led them through the foyer and kept a smile lacquered on his face until he'd shut the door behind them.

Outside, a cold drizzle was falling, transforming the Benbows' front path into a slick of sodden leaves, threatening to catch in the wheels of Sucram's chair. Across the street, Lenny Sand watched them from the front seat of his Buick. He drove off at high speed as they approached the curb.

"We tried, girls," said Lizzie's father. "That's all a person can do."

Julia and Lizzie never made another attempt to discover the contents of the sex offender's knapsack. Nor did Lizzie's father ever receive a phone call from Rex. When Lizzie reflected on the episode, which grew increasingly hazy with each passing year, what she remembered most vividly was neither the night of the break-in, nor the morning of the house call, but the afternoon following their visit, when Julia's father briefly laid siege to their own house.

The protesters carried signs reading "FOR SHAME" and "NIMBY" and—this placard held by a corn-fed young woman wearing a man's fishing hat—"PERVERTS OF A FEATHER FLOCK TOGETHER." They numbered about three dozen. Dr. Sand paced back and forth with a bullhorn, warning, "This is a family community, not a social experiment. Predators are not welcome here. Nobody has a right to welcome sex predators to our community." Two junior officers from the Pontefract police department sat guard on the Sucrams' porch. Myra ordered her daughters to remain inside and to stay away from the windows.

"I'm sorry you girls have to be exposed to this at your age," she said. "But they'll get tired and give up soon enough."

"I want to go out there," threatened Bill. "I won't be bullied in my own home by a pack of McCarthyites."

"Well, you can't," answered Lizzie's mother. "You're in no physical condition to take on a mob—and I'm not having you get yourself killed over nonsense." Myra stood behind her husband's chair and kneaded his shoulders. "Let them blow off their steam. What does it matter to us?"

"It's not nonsense," said Bill, but while he maneuvered his chair into the foyer, he made no effort to wheel himself onto the porch.

Lizzie waited for her father to drive off the protesters, and then she realized that her mother was also waiting, and her sister too, that they were all expecting her father to defy Myra's warning and take on the mob. But he didn't. Lizzie's father was now as much a prisoner inside his body as the sex offender was inside his grandmother's house, and Lizzie understood now that he truly was going to die. On impulse, she rushed toward him and wrapped her arms around his chest, pressing her head into his neck. That was the moment that would last with her—long after her mother resumed cooking meat, and Rex Benbow returned to prison, and Julia Sand choked to death on her own vomit in a motel room with an hourly rate. Lizzie would remember being thirteen years old, hugging her dying father, knowing that he was no longer the man who could fend off danger: it was the only thing that she could never forgive.

LA TRISTESSE DES HÉRISSONS

WE'D BEEN LIVING TOGETHER for eight months when we adopted the hedgehog. I'd wanted a German shepherd or a Doberman pinscher—a fearless, intimidating animal that could accompany me jogging in the park late at night. Adeline wanted a baby. Neither of us had ever mentioned anything about hedgehogs, but then Adeline read an article on unconventional pets, a throwaway piece in the back of a complimentary airline magazine, and soon enough I found myself wheeling a four-foot-long glass tank into the service elevator on a dolly. Hedgehogs require their space. It turned out that they also prefer warm, arid climates, so Adeline demanded that we install a convective heater and a dehumidifier in the living room. Outside, it was a balmy May in Manhattan. Inside, our apartment sweltered like the Kalahari.

Adeline named the hedgehog Orion. For three days, the prickly little devil entertained us by devouring mealworms and burrowing under aspen chips and exploring a makeshift maze that Adeline fashioned from cereal boxes. According to the *Happy Hedgehog Handbook*, responsible owners challenge their hogs with intellectual puzzles five times daily. My girlfriend followed the guide's countless dos and don'ts with a fundamentalist's zeal. Though I wasn't as smitten with the creature myself, I was delighted to see Adeline in such bright spirits for the first time since her mother's stroke. We didn't argue all weekend, and our sex life rekindled, although Adeline constantly reminded me to keep our volume at a minimum, fearful that an errant moan might alarm our barbed roommate. Actually, the word she used wasn't alarm. It was traumatize. I could envision her writing me up, just as she does the prospective parents she interviews during her home visits for the adoption agency: "Domicile unsuitable for placement. Poor boundary maintenance. Hedgehog likely to be exposed to sounds of sexual intercourse and to be emotionally traumatized." So I screwed like a deaf-mute.

Sunday was my late night at the restaurant. I co-own a bistro and wine bar with two of my former law school classmates, blood brothers in the fraternal order of ex-attorneys, and we take turns closing out the register. That evening, I returned home to find Adeline kneeling opposite Orion's cage, guarding the sleeping hedgehog with the intensity of a pediatric nurse. The ambient heat made even minor tasks like removing my raincoat feel like hard labor.

I kissed the top of Adeline's head. "You're up late."

"Can I ask you something?" she asked.

Her voice carried an ominous undertone—the same tone she'd used months earlier when accusing me of having an affair. "What's wrong?" I asked.

"Do you think he's depressed?"

It took me a moment to realize that she meant the hedgehog.

"What does he have to be depressed about?" I poured myself a shot of warm bourbon from the decanter on the sideboard. "He's got it damn good, if you ask me. No hawks or jackals to hide from. An endless supply of mealworms and crickets. The varmint has pretty much hit the hedgehog jackpot."

"I think he's depressed," said Adeline. "He looks depressed."

I did my connubial duty, placing my face inches from the glass cage and examining the hedgehog at eye level. As far as I could tell, Orion looked no different than he had the previous afternoon: languid, dopey, content. How could a creature be depressed when his brain was only the size of a kumquat?

"I'm really worried," said Adeline. "Mental illness is all too common in hedgehogs. I read an article online this morning."

I tapped the glass. Orion cocked his snout.

"We could take him back and get another one,"

I proposed.

I regretted the words as soon as they left my tongue.

"What the fuck is wrong with you?" snapped Adeline. "If you had a sick baby, you wouldn't take him back and get another one."

Good thing we have a hedgehog, I thought, and not a baby. But I had the sense to keep this sentiment to myself. Instead, I attempted to wrap my arm around Adeline's shoulders to comfort her. She shook me off.

"I can't take this, Josh. I just can't. Not on top of Mom," cried Adeline. "If he's not okay, I swear I'm going to jump out the window."

Adeline's threat was not an idle one. We lived on the sixth floor. When she thought I was cheating on her last February, she climbed out onto the ledge. After the police talked her down, she spent a week at Bellevue for observation.

My girlfriend's father hanged himself in a hotel closet when she was twelve years old. My own mother overdosed on Darvon when I was fourteen. Sometimes I wonder if a family history of suicide is a healthy foundation for a relationship, but couples have been drawn together by stranger bonds.

"I know what he needs," I declared, fishing a treat from the jar of freeze-dried silk worms. Orion explored the snack with the tip of his rhinarium and then ingested it with one swift gulp. "I think he's just hungry," I said. "For a hedgehog with depression, he's got an awfully hearty appetite."

"Hedgehog depression is atypical," replied Adeline.

"The worse they feel, the more they eat. In the wild, unhappy hedgehogs can consume their own body weight in locusts over the course of several hours . . . We'll have to keep him on a strict diet and weigh him at least twice a day."

"Sorry, buddy," I apologized to Orion. "But look on the bright side, Addy," I added. "That means more freeze-dried silk worms for us."

My girlfriend did not smile. "Don't be an asshole," she warned.

Adeline insisted we both skip work the next morning. That was easy enough for her—she works at a nonprofit—but both of my partners were out of town, so I had to reschedule job interviews with three prospective sous chefs and postpone the installation of chandeliers in the upstairs dining room. Instead, I accompanied my girlfriend to a high-end "veterinary psychiatrist" who had been featured on the cover of *New York Magazine*. Dr. Waller's office was located only blocks from the nursing home where Adeline's mother sat expressionless at the end of a musty corridor, periodically calling out lessons that she had memorized at Miss Porter's, where she'd once shared a swimming locker with the future Jacqueline Kennedy.

Our visits with Adeline's mother were short, somber, and all too frequent. Mrs. Terwilliger had not recognized us since her stroke in March, although she could still recite Matthew Arnold's "Dover Beach" and several soliloquies from *Measure for Measure*. That morning, she greeted us by shouting, "All Gaul is divided into three parts!" Adeline braided her mother's long silver hair while I sat on the window ledge with my hands in my pockets. My nostrils fought against the faint stench of urine. None of us spoke until we left, when Mrs. Terwilliger declared, "Of all three, the Belgae are the bravest, because they are farthest from civilization." By the time we arrived for our appointment with Dr. Waller, Adeline was in tears, and I'd resolved to shoot myself preemptively at age sixty-five.

Dr. Waller turned out to be a dapper and strikingly good-looking gentleman in his fifties who sported a silk magenta ascot under his burgundy jacket; a matching handkerchief protruded from his breast pocket. The therapist looked more like a game-show host than a veterinarian, and when he shook my hand—with a firm, no-nonsense grip—I was half expecting him to ask if I wished to buy a vowel.

He steered us into a spacious yet sterile office. A leather analyst's couch sat opposite Dr. Waller's desk. Two upholstered chairs faced the couch, surrounded by balls of yarn and artificial dog bones and a box of parrot snacks. Along one wall hung the therapist's diplomas: a medical degree from Yale, a veterinary degree from the University of New Hampshire, and an MBA from Duke. That was when I realized Waller treated both humans and animals in the same office—which helped explain his $400 cash only fee for an initial consultation. Adeline completed a questionnaire while I wrote the headshrinker a check, impulsively jotting "quackery" on the memo line. Then I inked out "quackery" and wrote "relationship counseling" in the margin above. Dr. Waller pocketed the check without even glancing at it.

He perused the questionnaire for several minutes, nodding and sighing as though depressed hedgehogs were the marrow of his business. When at last he looked up, his sympathetic eyes focused entirely on Adeline. "I am so sorry Orion is having such a hard time," he said, speaking of the animal like a beloved mutual friend. "As best as you can, dear, try to tell me when you first noticed something was amiss . . ."

Adeline related how she'd come to check on Orion before breakfast on Sunday morning and realized that he "just wasn't himself." She mentioned his increased appetite, changes in his sleeping habits, and his loss of interest in his exercise wheel. Dr. Waller scrawled notes on a legal pad. Once, he interrupted Adeline to ask a series of precise questions about the hedgehog's bowel patterns, but for the most part he merely offered my girlfriend a smile of boundless sympathy. When Adeline finished her narrative, concluding with a tangent about how she'd lost a guinea pig to pneumonia in her childhood, along with a confession that she didn't handle these tragedies well, Dr. Waller capped his pen and shifted his attention to me.

"Is there anything you'd like to add, Mr. Barrow?"

He'd caught me off guard—speculating to myself about his annual income—so I said the first thing that popped into my consciousness. "When we bring the hedgehog for his therapy," I asked, "will you have him lie down on the couch?"

Adeline shot me a venomous look. Dr. Waller frowned.

"You will not bring the hedgehog here. Ever," he replied earnestly. "I treat canines in this office, Mr. Barrow. Your animal is already suffering. Do you want to compound his depression with post-traumatic stress?"

I refused to meet Dr. Waller's gaze. I found myself wishing that I was a hedgehog myself at that moment, so that I might curl into a protective ball. Eventually, I sensed that the therapist had turned his focus back toward Adeline.

"So you agree that he's depressed?" she asked.

"That's most likely. You should certainly take him to his regular vet to rule out organic causes—thyroid disease, paraneoplastic syndromes. But it does indeed sound like a mood phenomenon. La tristesse des hérissons, as the French say. The sadness of the hedgehogs." He gave the diagnosis a fatal ring. "Psychosis is common in hedgehogs. Depression far less so. But we have to take our patients as we find them, I suppose."

Dr. Waller offered Adeline a tissue to dab her eyes.

Adeline composed herself. "So what can we do?" she asked.

The therapist didn't respond at once, but gazed thoughtfully into the ether like a magician pausing before pulling off a particularly dazzling trick.

"We don't know much—yet—about mood phenomena in hedgehogs," he said, "but what limited understanding we do have strongly suggests that patients improve with increased levels of comfort. So my best advice is to hold Orion on your lap, read to him daily . . . Let him grow accustomed to your scents, to the sounds of your voices . . ."

That was too much for me—and it even crossed my mind that I was on some newfangled version of *Candid Camera.*

"Let me get this straight. You want us to read to the hedgehog?"

"It's not about what I want or don't want," Dr. Waller replied calmly. "It's about what will help Orion become more relaxed in his new home."

"And my reading him bedtime stories is going to relax him?"

"It will help. I'm also going to start him on five milligrams of Prozac daily."

Dr. Waller scribbled the prescription on his pad and handed it to Adeline.

"Check in with me next week. If he's not feeling any better by then, we can add a low dose of Wellbutrin or Abilify as an adjunctive agent."

A man in a relationship has to choose his battles wisely, so that afternoon I made a point of reading aloud to the hedgehog. I spread a pair of bath towels over my lap and scooped up the thorny lump of a creature with a heavy oven mitt. After twenty minutes, he slowly uncoiled and began to lather saliva over his back with his tongue. Adeline poked her head into the living room periodically, probably to make sure I hadn't decided to practice juggling with the varmint. Once she gave me a thumbs up. It struck me that if I ever wanted to have a child, few women would have as much love to offer as Adeline. But she was already thirty-six—and I was barely ready to commit to raising a house pet with an average life span of less than three years.

Not much has been written for or about hedgehogs, but I did manage to find a copy of Isaiah Berlin's *The Hedgehog and the Fox* among my old college books. When I tired of philosophy, which occurred rather quickly, I read to Orion about the adventures of Stickly-Prickly in Kipling's "The Beginning of the Armadillos." Choosing hedgehog-themed works was entirely to amuse myself, I recognized. As far as my audience was concerned, I might just as well have read names from the telephone directory. Orion passed most of the day sprawled on the towels, anointing his spikes with hog-spittle, interrupted only by my trips to the restroom and his to the litter box. I was on the verge of quitting for the day when Adeline stormed into the living room.

"You've got to be kidding me."

She yanked the book from my hands. Carroll's *Alice in Wonderland*.

"What's wrong?" I asked, sincerely puzzled.

"What's wrong? What's wrong?" demanded Adeline. "I could hear you from the kitchen . . . Do you really think this is appropriate reading material for him?"

I'd been narrating the episode in Alice where the Queen of Hearts plays croquet, using flamingos as mallets and hedgehogs for balls. Before I'd owned a hedgehog, the full humor of that match hadn't been apparent to me. Of course, the large snifter of Chivas Regal that I'd polished off might also have played a role in my amusement.

"Who cares what I read?" I shot back. "Jesus, Addy. He's only a hedgehog. He can't understand a word I'm saying."

"He can understand the tone. He can sense whether you're showing him affection or mocking him." Adeline swaddled one of the bath towels around the animal and cradled him against her chest like an infant. "It's going to be okay, darling," she cooed. "You're a loved hedgehog, aren't you?"

"I wasn't mocking him," I said. "I was trying to be culturally relevant."

"Okay, let's not fight," said Adeline. "I'm sorry I jumped on you like that. Anyway, I think it's past hedgehog bedtime . . . Why don't you run down to the pharmacy before it gets too late?"

I didn't argue. I was actually rather inebriated and glad to escape the torrid apartment for a few minutes, so I took the opportunity to stroll past the bistro, curious to see whether our Monday night happy hour was drawing an early crowd. It wasn't. Then I walked another three blocks to a chain drugstore that I'd never before visited, not wanting our local CVS to get the wrong idea about the Prozac. I knew I'd drunk too much, because my ulcer was flaring up.

The pharmacist was an elderly, flat-faced man with an Eastern European accent and the bedside manner of a Stasi agent. I handed the script across the counter.

He grinned knowingly. "You got insurance?"

"It's not for me," I said, struggling not to slur my words. "It's for a hedgehog."

"That's a good one," said the pharmacist.

"It's true," I insisted. "Could I really make that up?"

"And let me guess. The hedgehog is uninsured."

"I'm afraid so," I conceded.

The pharmacist disappeared behind a partition. Moments later, I heard laughter from the interior of the shop. Fifteen minutes elapsed before the old man returned with a small paper bag. "That will be $148.52," he said. "You'd better hope that hedgehog of yours lays golden eggs."

I held my tongue and forked over my credit card.

"Do me a favor, buddy," he said. "Tell the hedgehog that he may experience insomnia, nausea, and headache."

"Will do."

"And fluoxetine can kill his sex life," added the pharmacist.

The old man didn't realize how off the mark he was. In reality, I'd be sleeping in the living room until the Prozac worked its magic.

"Not this hedgehog, buddy. This hedgehog's got a pecker the size of a Louisville slugger," I announced, yanking the bag of pills from the pharmacist's grasp. "Do me a favor. Tell your pill-pushing buddies behind the wall that the last guy who laughed at this hedgehog ended up short a set of kneecaps."

I staggered onto the sidewalk, aglow with delight and liquor: if I couldn't mock my own hedgehog, I told myself, nobody could.

&

Our regimen of bedtime stories and antidepressants drove the hedgehog's depression into rapid remission over the course of the next week—or, at least, that was the shared perception of Adeline and Dr. Waller. All I noticed was that the creature consumed fewer moth larvae. Otherwise, he remained his stolid and inscrutable self, curling and uncurling to his own internal whims, although after six days of medication, he did display a renewed interest in his exercise wheel. And while I couldn't detect Orion's psychiatric progress directly, I witnessed his recovery reflected in Adeline's mood, which improved steadily with every vicarious Prozac. By June, she was once again the vibrant, laugh-prone beauty I'd fallen in love with three years earlier in the St. Vincent's Hospital emergency room, where I'd accompanied her—mostly for fear of litigation—after she'd tripped over a poorly placed dessert cart and fractured her ankle. Instead of suing, she'd invited me to a picnic in Union Square.

I no longer saw the point of reading to the hedgehog. On the tenth evening of my literary therapy, I dared to suggest as much to Adeline. We were ensconced on the sofa in the living room, her legs swung over my lap so that I could massage her feet through her stockings. Across the room, the hedgehog galloped like a mechanical toy on his exercise wheel, generating a reassuring metallic whir.

"It's amazing what half a bottle of Prozac can do," I mused. "Listen to him go. What a shame we can't harness all that energy, use it to power the lights." I traced my fingers along Adeline's toes, yearning to kick-start our sex life. "Do you think they have marathons for hedgehogs?"

Adeline slid her foot from my grip. "I'm worried," she said.

"What is there to worry about?"

"All that running isn't healthy," Adeline replied. "Hedgehogs aren't supposed to run marathons." She climbed down onto the carpet and attempted to distract Orion from his workout, but the animal maintained the focus of a trained athlete. Even pounding on the glass didn't sidetrack him. Rather than balling up when she reached into his cage, he hissed at her and held his ground.

"Something's terribly wrong," said Adeline. "Frankly, I think he's gone manic."

"You're joking."

"Do I sound like I'm joking, Josh? There's a warning about risk of mania on the package insert for the Prozac. If it can happen to people, why shouldn't it happen to hedgehogs?"

I didn't have an answer—but I sensed this wasn't going to be the last time Adeline raised precisely that question. I could already picture my girlfriend driving a station wagon with a bumper sticker that read: *Hedgehogs are people, too.*

Adeline was still on the rug, scrutinizing Orion. Every few moments, she tried to caress him with her mitted hand, withdrawing her fingers only after he dug his tiny teeth into the Kevlar.

"Promise me he's going to be okay," she pleaded. "Please, Josh."

"I promise we'll do everything we can," I agreed.

"Everything" necessitated another morning away from the restaurant, another session with the enlightened and costly Dr. Waller. As we waited in the therapist's vestibule, I found myself reflecting that I should have given in to Adeline about the baby—because if we'd spent a fortune taking care of a sick infant, at the end of the day at least we'd have had a child. In contrast, no matter how much time and money and emotional energy we devoted to Orion, the most we could ever expect to end up with was an obtuse creature that smelled like rotting mulch.

The door to Dr. Waller's inner sanctum opened, and a middle-aged woman hiding behind a kerchief and sunglasses exited quickly. Her handbag was slung across one shoulder; atop her other shoulder perched a red-faced lovebird. It crossed my mind that the pair might be receiving family counseling, and I couldn't help grinning. At that moment, Dr. Waller beckoned us into his office.

"Is something humorous, Mr. Barrow?" inquired the therapist.

"Not at all," I said quickly.

"Humor is a universal emotion," said Dr. Waller. "All mammals have a rudimentary sense of humor. And humor has a great deal of therapeutic potential. The challenge, of course, is how to tap into it. What a human being finds funny will necessarily differ from what a raccoon or a muskrat finds funny."

"Obviously," I said.

Dr. Waller eyed me warily, like a general preparing to reprimand a junior officer, but ultimately he allowed my remark to pass. The therapist toyed with an unlit pipe and listened as my girlfriend recounted our latest tale of hedgehog woe.

"He's out of control," Adeline concluded. "He has no judgment anymore. To be honest, I'm afraid he might do something dangerous."

"Let's hope it doesn't come to that," soothed Dr. Waller. "I think it's rather clear that the antidepressant has tipped him into mania. It happens. It cannot be helped. Fortunately, as the Prozac leaves his system, there's a good chance his mood will restabilize on its own."

"And what if it doesn't?" demanded Adeline.

"That's where environmental factors come into play," explained Dr. Waller. "Sensory overstimulation can exacerbate bipolar disorder in many species. I've seen it in rabbits. I've seen it in hamsters. While I've never seen it in hedgehogs myself, there are case reports in the literature . . . I can prescribe twenty-five milligrams of lithium twice daily, if Orion will take it, but what he really requires is a stimulus-free atmosphere."

"We'll do whatever you suggest," said Adeline.

I sensed that the therapist was leading us toward a precipice. "What exactly do you mean by stimulus free?" I asked.

"No loud sounds, no pungent aromas," said Dr. Waller. "But you don't have to go overboard. Hedgehogs don't actually hear or smell as well as most people believe. Vision is by far their strongest sensory modality," he added. "If you want to break Orion's mania, you'll have to keep him in compete darkness."

"For how long?" I asked.

"Until he recovers," said Dr. Waller. "It could be days . . . it could be months. It all depends upon the hedgehog."

Adeline thanked the therapist profusely. I wrote another $200 check.

Outside, Union Square was alive with rhododendrons and forsythias, the cheerful throngs of NYU undergraduates and lunching office workers a striking contrast to the elderly captives we'd soon confront at Mrs. Terwilliger's nursing home. It seemed so long ago that Adeline and I had picnicked in that same park, opposite the statue of Lafayette—so long ago when I'd markered the words "If you sue me, I'll still like you" on Adeline's cast. I longed to remind her of that distant afternoon but feared that, in her present state of mind, the memory might actually upset her.

"Maybe this hedgehog is too much for us," I ventured. "Maybe he's too sick to be raised outside a medical setting."

"Don't you dare say that ever again," said Adeline, her voice like a stiletto. "If he's too much for you, I'm too much for you. We're a package deal."

⛥

If it had been entirely up to me, we'd have punched a few air holes through a shoebox and slid Orion into a bureau drawer until his mania subsided. Needless to say, the decision was not entirely up to me, so I spent the greater part of the next eight hours light-proofing our apartment while Adeline tended to the hedgehog in a rented darkroom at the Manhattan Institute of Photography. She was determined that Orion was to retain free roam of his cage while under light quarantine, which meant that all of the living room windows had to be papered over with black oaktag board. And that was just the start of my efforts. I sealed off the bottom of the apartment door with a strip of rubber, moved all the small appliances into our bedroom, and hung a damask curtain across the foyer entrance. Love sometimes requires a willingness to indulge unreasonable requests, and I was determined to blot every last photon from our lives to soothe Adeline's nerves.

I sipped Canadian whiskey while I labored. Okay, maybe I enjoyed a few sips too many, but the Glen Breton was surprisingly smooth—so much so that I downed half a bottle over the course of several hours. I'd been drinking more heavily ever since Adeline had accused me of sleeping with one of our college-aged waitresses, because while the charge itself was 100 percent false, I still felt guilty that I'd found the young coed attractive—and even guiltier that I'd terminated her so abruptly. But Adeline had stopped by the bistro one evening, on her way home from her office, and she'd seen the two of us sharing a plate of calamari at the bar. To quote my girlfriend's own words, "I don't care if anything actually happened. What matters is how I felt when I saw you." So I fired the girl, and Adeline climbed out onto the sixth-story ledge. After her stint in Bellevue, she never mentioned the incident again.

I'd just taped over the red light on the carbon-monoxide detector when Adeline returned home, wheeling Orion's travel case in a stroller. She immediately shut the door behind her and flipped off the overhead lights. Darkness cloaked the room. I had to feel my way down from the stepstool.

"Dark enough for you?" I asked.

"More than dark enough," said Adeline.

"I'd kiss you right now, only I don't think I could find you."

I heard the squeak of stroller wheels and the frenetic scampering of the hedgehog inside his case.

"You're going to kill me for this, Josh, but I have to ask," said Adeline. "They're selling fresh-cut lilacs on the corner. I didn't want to buy them while I had Orion with me on account of the smell . . . Would you be all right taking care of him for an hour while I take a bouquet of lilacs to Mama? You know how she loves lilacs."

"Go. Don't think twice," I said. "Orion and I will do some male bonding."

"Thank you!" declared Adeline. "I'll be as quick as I can."

Her footsteps inched back into the entryway. When she opened the apartment door, the light from the corridor limned her silhouette angelically. "Make sure you don't let him out unless you have the lights off," Adeline warned. "And no silk worms before bedtime. They'll give him indigestion."

"Everything is under control," I assured her.

And then she was gone, and I was alone with the hedgehog.

I turned on the fluorescent lights in the kitchen, illuminating the living room just enough for me to unload the hedgehog safely. I realized that Adeline would have viewed this as cheating—as a direct assault on the creature's welfare—but I wasn't about to carry a manic animal with a pelt of spikes across our apartment in the dark. I probably would have turned the overhead lights on, too, but I was afraid that Adeline might be testing me—waiting on the sidewalk outside to spy for cracks of light around the oaktag. To my surprise, Orion appeared to have burned through his mania already. He didn't resist when I cupped him into the mitt and set him down inside his cage. It only took a few seconds for him to uncoil and cuddle into his woodchips.

My ulcer was burning again—like a sharp quill being driven through my abdomen—so I retreated into the kitchen and poured myself a glass of milk. I sipped slowly, letting the cool liquid coat my throat and esophagus. When I returned to the living room, the hedgehog lay tucked into a mound of chips, sleeping soundly. It was only seven o'clock, but as far as I was concerned, the creature had the right idea. I poured myself a second glass of milk, turned off the kitchen light, and went to bed.

☙

I dreamed the world was an overfed hedgehog, that all of humanity lived its existence, oblivious, at the tip of one long quill. At some point, Dr. Waller tried to push me off the edge of that quill into the abyss—and I awoke to Adeline, attempting to drag me off the bed by my feet. "You're a total asshole, a total fucking asshole," she shouted. "I knew I couldn't trust you!"

"What's going on?"

"How stupid do you think I am?" continued Adeline, pulling my sock from my foot. "You promised me you wouldn't expose Orion to any light. You promised me everything was under control."

"Everything is under control."

"Then how do you explain this?"

She held up the empty milk glass I'd left on the bedside table.

"You poured yourself a glass of milk after you put Orion in his cage," she said. "Don't you lie to me, Josh. I know you let him out first—before you got the milk."

"So?"

"So you didn't take the light bulb out of the goddam refrigerator," she cried. "I don't care how little light he was actually exposed to. That's not the point. The point is that you're careless, and selfish, and you don't give a damn about either of us."

The room slowly came into focus. I was still somewhat drunk, but also mildly hungover—an all-too-toxic mix. "So I don't give a damn about you, do I?"

"Apparently not." Adeline started punching my hip, my ribs; she pounded the side of my mouth. "I ask you to do one small thing, just one tiny damn thing, and you can't even do that. What is wrong with you?"

I'm not sure what finally drove me to the edge—the pain in my jaw, or the alcohol, or some inexplicable force that controls the lives of hedgehog and man. All I can say is that something snapped. I charged into the living room, flipped on the overhead lights, and as soon as I'd managed to squeeze my hand into an oven mitt, I scooped up the dumbstruck hedgehog. Adeline was hollering, sobbing, pleading. I don't think she realized my intentions until I'd yanked down the oaktag board and was already climbing out onto the window ledge—and by then she was powerless to stop me.

Wind gusted up the avenue. Below, traffic lights stretched across the city in beads of red and green like strings of Christmas decorations.

I didn't have a plan—not exactly. A part of me yearned to grasp the hedgehog like a baseball and heave it into the sea of yellow cabs below, and another part of me realized that was an insane idea, and yet a third part of me wanted to hurl the damn animal downward with full force and then dive after it. So I stood there, paralyzed. Drunk. Angry. Lost. Adeline poked her head out the window, but I couldn't hear what she was saying. When she started climbing onto the ledge, I inched myself farther along the brick-face. Some couple we made, the pair of us fifty yards above the street, one hollering and the other clasping a hedgehog.

That was when I lost my grip on the creature. Its quills slipped without warning from the Kevlar mitt. Instinctively, I reached out with my other hand—my bare hand—and clasped my naked fingers around the thorny, squirming ball. I was far too smashed to feel much pain, but I could sense the warmth of the blood trickling down my wrist and under my sleeve. I suppose the blood reminded me of how close we all are to the abyss, how easily a guy can step over the edge. It was the blood that kept me from letting go, that kept me clinging to that hedgehog for dear life.

STRINGS

RABBI CYNTHIA FELDER WAS NEWLY MARRIED, and in her pulpit only six months, when a former lover asked to borrow the sanctuary. In the past, she had loaned out the synagogue's banquet hall generously—to a mixer for gay and lesbian Jewish singles, even as a temporary gathering place for a congregation of Korean Presbyterians burned from their church—but welcoming strangers into the tabernacle itself was quite another matter. A Reform shul was still a shul, after all. To conduct Caesar's business in the shadow of the Pentateuch scrolls strained even Cynthia's liberalism. Yet for Jacques Krentz, the forty-eight-year-old, chronically underemployed composer, second-wave beatnik, and avowed agnostic with whom Cynthia had once briefly shared a futon, only that hallowed chamber would do.

"Four hundred cellos," declared Jacques, painting this image on the air with a sweep of his open palms. "What kind of banquet hall has acoustics fit for four hundred cellos? If I wanted a banquet hall, I'd have called the Knights of Columbus."

Jacques had presented himself without warning, sauntering into Cynthia's office while her elderly receptionist was on a bathroom break. He sported khaki knee-shorts, Birkenstocks, and a mischievous grin. Eight years had passed since she'd last laid eyes on him. Back then, she had been freshly minted from Barnard, working through her post-college bewilderment as a publicist at the Jewish Museum, and Jacques, pushing forty, had likely been the most gifted musician ever to vend hot dogs at Yankee Stadium. Now she led her own congregation on Central Park West, and he sold cotton candy from a cart at the South Street Seaport. Nevertheless, he still flashed the enthusiasm of the master impresario. Although Jacques was only a few inches taller than Cynthia, and of modest build, the rabbi's excessively furnished, book-lined chamber could hardly contain the composer's nervous vigor. He paced the carpet as he bargained with her, as though galvanized by an electrical current, pressing his fingertips into his balding scalp.

"It's only for a few hours, Cynth," he emphasized. "We rehearse here until noon, then we go out to the park and perform the concert. You'll hardly notice we're here."

"God will notice you're here."

Jacques shrugged. "Maybe God sleeps late," he said.

"Besides, it's a Sunday. If He is awake, won't He be hanging out with Catholics?"

That was enough to remind Cynthia why her relationship with the composer had gone south. It hadn't been the age difference or the education gap—or even his habit of inviting her out to dinner and then asking her to pick up the tab. What had undone them was her ex-lover's blatant contempt for anything remotely theological.

Jacques leaned over Cynthia's desk, bracing his arms against the blotter. "Look, Cynth. This is a matter of professional life and death for me," he pleaded. "I've even talked the classical music critic from the *Times* into coming . . . She's the second-string critic, but still." An aura of helplessness penetrated the composer's bravado. "I haven't asked you for anything since we split up, have I? Honestly, this could be my last chance to make my mark."

Cynthia had heard such claims before. At the same time, she did not like to think of herself as impeding another human being's happiness. She tried for a moment to blot out their past relationship, to view her ex-lover as King Solomon might: a stranger presenting an ethical conundrum. The composer's dark eyes beseeched her. Through the open window drifted the shouts of children from the neighboring school yard.

"Okay," she agreed. "But only for three hours. And no food in the sanctuary."

"I knew you'd come through," declared Jacques, glowing again. "Three hours and not a second more," he promised, extending an invitation to her and her husband for the actual concert in Central Park. "You'll come, won't you?"

"I guess so," she said. "But I can't speak for Jed."

"If you weren't a married woman," said Jacques, "I swear I'd kiss you."

Cynthia sensed that he might have kissed her anyway, had she allowed it. When he finally left her office—promising to say "ten thousand Hail Marys in Hebrew"—she felt as though she'd narrowly dodged a bolt of lightning.

ॐ

She'd been drafting her sermon that morning, as she did every Monday, but Jacques' appearance had derailed her efforts. Unable to refocus, she retrieved her purse from her desk drawer and told Marsha she'd be breaking for an early lunch. Outside, the spring day was a cloud of pollen and humidity. Daffodils blanketed the gentle slopes along either side of the park's wrought-iron gates. Alongside a sign warning against feeding pigeons, a badger-faced man in a paperboy cap tossed bread crusts to a conclave of birds. Cynthia cut a brisk course through the greenery, past the concrete pavilion where Jacques was to marshal his battalion of cellos, and emerged onto Fifth Avenue just as the bells of the Russian Orthodox Church tolled noon. She entered her husband's waiting room unannounced—admitted by a departing brunette whose reflective sunglasses recalled the heroines of 1970s spy thrillers. The only other patient in the lobby, a middle-aged woman with a facial tic, eyed

Cynthia warily over a weight-loss magazine. She appeared fearful that the rabbi might steal her appointment.

Cynthia seated herself on an upholstered chair. Then she thought better of waiting and knocked on the door of her husband's inner office. The woman with the facial tic glowered ten million plagues at her.

"It's me," said the rabbi. "Are you alone?"

Cynthia's husband opened the door, and she slid past him into his psychiatric sanctum. Jed Levin's collage of diplomas—Harvard College, Yale Medical School, countless board certifications—would have drawn out even Freud's inadequacies. Yet the soft-spoken analyst who poked his head into the lobby, placating his waiting patient, was incomparably more humble than many less-credentialed men Cynthia had dated over the years. He followed her into the office and settled down beside her on the leather couch—as though they were both patients, being treated by an invisible therapist.

"So what's going on?" asked Jed. "Are you all right?"

"I think so," she answered. "I don't know . . . I mean, I should be fine . . . but I'm not."

The truth was that she felt much worse than not fine. She felt as though a cluster of land mines had detonated inside her skull. Somehow, a glass of cool water ended up clasped between her trembling hands, and she sipped gratefully.

"Is anybody dead or injured?" asked Jed.

Cynthia shook her head.

"Then it's nothing that can't be fixed," he assured

her. "Trust me, honey. It's much better to not be okay when you ought to be fine, than to be perfectly content when you really should be falling to pieces. The people that nothing ever fazes are the ones who truly frighten me." Jed's delicate fingers brushed the bangs from Cynthia's eyes. "Now take a deep breath and tell me what's wrong."

"Four hundred cellos," she answered. And she related how Jacques had bamboozled the sanctuary from her. "It's part of some city-wide festival," she explained, although she was vague herself about the details. "There's going to be a symphony for seventy-six trombones on the steps of City Hall . . . and an all-bagpipe parade drill . . . and the woman organizing the bassoons is trying to set an international record. She's going to have two thousand bassoonists playing 'Somewhere Over the Rainbow' on the boardwalk at Coney Island. You're not upset with me, are you?"

"Why should I be upset?"

"I thought you might be. Jacques has a history with me, after all."

"Do I have anything to be upset about?" asked Jed.

"Of course not. Not even remotely."

"Good. Then I'm not upset."

Jed smiled at her affectionately. Soon his smile broadened into a grin and finally erupted into red-faced laughter.

"What's so funny?" demanded Cynthia.

Her husband fought to regain his breath. "Nothing," he gasped. "Nothing."

"You're not laughing at me, are you?"

Jed shook his head. "I don't know why I'm laughing. It's not funny at all," he said. "It's actually somewhat horrific . . . But the idea just popped into my head that if there were a natural disaster while those gazillion bassoonists are gathered together—an earthquake or a terrorist attack or something—that could wipe out all of the bassoon players in the entire country. We would have a worldwide bassoonist shortage. A bassoonist famine!"

Her husband's amusement took hold of her, too. She hugged his arm.

"You're demented," she said, "but I love you."

"I love you, too," he replied. "Now go write your sermon and give Mrs. Marcus out there a chance to tell me what she's planning for her reincarnation."

The subject of Cynthia's sermon, inspired by that week's parashah on levirate marriage, was to be the romance of Ruth and Boaz. She'd intended to launch her talk with a quotation extolling the power of love to bridge rival traditions, words she still recalled from her own childhood Sunday school class, but a quick search of the Internet revealed that the passage she had admired actually referred to Antony and Cleopatra. So she was gazing at a blank computer screen the following afternoon—her desk strewn with Talmudic commentaries and newspaper articles and even a book of *New Yorker* wedding cartoons—when she heard the gravelly rasp of Marsha Pastarnack threatening to telephone security. An instant later, Jacques Krentz strolled through Cynthia's open door without so much as a knock. "You can't go in there, sir," the elderly receptionist called after him. She appeared ashen-faced in the doorframe, phone in hand, entreating her employer for guidance and forgiveness.

"It's all right, Marsha," Cynthia reassured her. "He's an old friend."

The receptionist surveyed Jacques doubtfully but retreated to her cubicle. Cynthia crossed to the door and shut it firmly. "If you ever do that again," she said, "I will have Marsha call security. You can't just storm in here like an invading army."

Jacques didn't even acknowledge her frustration. He picked up one of the articles on her desk at random and skimmed it: a *National Geographic* clipping about cultures in which teenage girls symbolically marry trees. "What are you working on?" he asked.

"Didn't you hear a word I said?" countered Cynthia. "You have absolutely no business upsetting poor Marsha like that."

Marsha Pastarnack had been the previous rabbi's sister-in-law, and after his death Cynthia had felt obliged to keep her on. The receptionist's only formal qualification for her job was a six-week course in Gregg shorthand that dated back to the Eisenhower administration, but she kept the office festive with homegrown bouquets and hand-crafted origami fowl.

"I certainly didn't mean to upset anyone," said

Jacques. "But I hope that you do think of me as an old friend, because I really need your help."

Many people asked Cynthia for assistance each day—congregants hoping for a hospital visit or a personal blessing or a dose of Biblical wisdom. Fulfilling these mitzvahs was what the rabbi treasured most about her calling. Yet the same request for aid, coming from Jacques, forced her to suppress her temper. She had tried to fix the composer's life one too many times in the past—ordering him college catalogs, securing him a job interview at her uncle's advertising agency—and he'd long ago exhausted her reserve of goodwill. The appalling truth was that she'd once loved Jacques Krentz, this ne'er-do-well with his premature comb-over and unifying theory of the arts, but now his presence in her office simply piqued her frustration.

"Another favor?" she asked.

"I know this may sound absurd," said Jacques, "but it turns out that the city doesn't provide any chairs for the concert."

"That's unfortunate," replied Cynthia.

Jacques waited for her to say more, but she didn't. She was determined not to make their encounter easy for him. Eventually, he sighed, as though accepting an inevitable torture, and he asked, "Is there any chance I could borrow four hundred folding chairs this Sunday?"

"You're incorrigible," answered Cynthia. "I don't see you for eight years, and now you've asked me for two favors in two days. Seriously, Jacques. What would you do if I said no?"

"I swear I won't ask you for anything else," he said. "The cellists will carry the chairs to the park with them after the rehearsal, and they'll bring them back by five o'clock. You have my word." The composer rubbed his jaw thoughtfully before adding, "This isn't only about helping me. It's about the music. Can you imagine the grandeur of four hundred cellos playing simultaneously? A cello concert of this size has only been attempted once before ever—at St. Mark's in 1974—but Cardinal Luciani of Venice limited the orchestra to liturgical compositions. On Sunday, we're going to perform Bartok, Schoenberg, John Cage . . . Luciani would roll over in his papal grave."

Jacques waved his arms above his head with the enthusiasm of an evangelist. "And if you say no, I'll have to cancel the entire event . . . I already looked into other options for seating. You have no idea how much it costs to rent a folding chair."

Nor did Jacques, she recognized. She was certain he hadn't actually made the slightest inquiry about chair rentals, but that was beside the point. She didn't begrudge him the chairs. What bothered Cynthia was the sense that she was being played the fool—that the composer thought he was convincing her to sponsor the musical equivalent of stone soup. But if she accused him of nickel-and-diming her now, when he'd known all along that he'd come back for more, she knew he'd deny it.

"I suppose you might as well take the chairs," she conceded. "But to be quite honest, I'm not sure if we even have four hundred."

"You have more than five hundred, in fact," answered Jacques. "I took a peek downstairs in your banquet hall earlier this morning, and I counted them."

Cynthia presided over a graveside service in New Jersey that afternoon, for a widowed kindergarten teacher who, in retirement, had illustrated the synagogue's newsletter, and the rabbi returned from the cemetery with a bad case of gloom. In the rail tunnel beneath the Hudson, and again during her stroll up Broadway to their Morningside Heights brownstone, her mind replayed the morning's conversation with Jacques, and not once did she loan him the chairs.

Jed was already cooking dinner when she arrived home. Even from the second-story landing, she could smell the buttery aroma of his trademark grouper patties. Not many husbands would choose to end a workday in rolled shirtsleeves and a floral-print apron—and even fewer looked so handsome in their domesticity. During Jacques' months on Cynthia's futon, the composer had subsisted mainly on carry out chow mein and chocolate bars.

Jed set down his potato-filled skillet just long enough to peck her on the lips. "I couldn't find any nutmeg in the cupboard, so I went out on a limb and sprinkled in some paprika. If it's a complete disaster, we can always splurge on that new bistro," he said. "Also, your dentist called. Apparently, you skipped your cleaning this afternoon."

She had missed her appointment. Because she was

frazzled. Because Jacques Krentz and his army of cellos had addled her brain.

"Who gives a damn about clean teeth?" she snapped. "I hope they all fall out."

"If you insist," replied Jed. "But if you cancel twenty-four hours in advance next time, we'll save eighty-five dollars."

Cynthia's husband scooped up a grouper fillet with his spatula and slapped it onto a waiting plate. The fish sizzled, bleeding juice. Cynthia rummaged inside her purse for a Tylenol but found only an empty plastic bottle. She'd already exhausted the supply of painkillers in the medicine cabinet the previous evening, and her headache wasn't yet worth a trip to the corner drugstore. Instead, she poured herself a tall glass of iced tea.

"I saw Jacques again today," she announced. "He wanted chairs."

"Chairs?"

"Folding chairs. For the cellists."

Saying this aloud made the request sound far too reasonable. Why shouldn't an old friend ask to borrow seats for his concert? By objective standards, nothing that Jacques Krentz had done merited her degree of anxiety. Nonetheless, Cynthia felt as though she could bite into her glass. "Don't you want to know if I gave him the chairs?" she asked.

"Sure," agreed Jed. "Did you give him the chairs?"

"Yes, I gave him the goddam chairs," she shot back. The sharp tone of her own voice surprised her.

Jed turned off the gas range and set down his spatula.

"I'm sorry," said Cynthia. "It's not you that I'm upset at. It's me . . . I don't know why I keep letting that man get to me."

A gray twilight had been seeping across the kitchen, but she hadn't bothered to flip on the overhead light. Her husband circled behind her and caressed her shoulders.

"You know what I'm going to say, honey, so there's probably no point in me saying it," Jed said. "But I'm going to say it anyway." His caress drifted into a massage. "I wish you'd at least think about talking to someone. Not forever. Maybe just for a handful of sessions. You'd be surprised what a few hours of therapy can do for you."

"I've already thought about seeing someone," she replied, soothed for the time being by his confident touch. "But that's you, Jed. Not me. I came across this Talmudic commentary a few days ago about a religious man, a hacham, who pulls a thread on his tallis, and all of the prayer shawls in the entire community unravel. Does that make sense?"

"More or less."

Cynthia's own life felt wound tightly—Jacques would say too tightly—into a functional albeit highly tangled spool. "I'm not ready to start yanking threads," she said. "Please don't ask me to."

"I suppose I tried my best," answered her husband. "But I'm sorry you have to go through all of this. Remind me: when is this concert?"

"Sunday afternoon. I assume you don't want to go."

"Why not?" asked Jed. "I've never heard four hundred

cellos before."

She hadn't expected this—not even from Jed. If his ex-girlfriend ever conducted four hundred cellos in a nearby park, she'd have hid under her bed with earplugs.

"Jacques is actually quite talented," said Cynthia, her muscles relaxing under her husband's firm kneading. "As hopeless and impractical as any man in the world, but extremely talented nonetheless. I suppose the show might turn out brilliantly."

"Thanks to your folding chairs," replied Jed. "Just think of it, honey. If this concert transforms your friend into the next Toscanini, your small contribution will be a grand footnote in the annals of twenty-first century music." He kissed the back of her head. "Now would you rather have chardonnay or sauvignon vert with the grouper?"

Wednesday passed, and then Thursday, with no further signs of Jacques. Cynthia completed a final draft of her sermon—on the eight specific musical instruments mentioned by name in the Old Testament and the Mishna's commentaries on the First Temple's orchestra. How easy it was to forget that the original Israelites' services had been punctuated by the whistles of the halil flute and the delightful patter of the tof drum. Her own synagogue confined the musical accompaniment to Cantor Lustgarten's chants and the sobs of hungry infants.

Cynthia had been on edge ever since she'd ceded the

folding chairs, knowing deep down that Jacques might have further requests tucked away, but when Friday arrived without another appearance, she sensed her blood pressure returning to its baseline. By the time she taught her introductory Yiddish course that afternoon, she'd nearly forgotten her earlier stress. She was already packing up her laptop, looking forward to her weekly Sabbath dinner in Brooklyn with Jed and her in-laws, when the composer rapped his fist on her doorframe. He wore a baseball cap and a five o'clock shadow.

"Thank God I caught you," he declared. "I realized on the way here that I don't even know your home phone number anymore."

"Good Shabbos to you, too," said Cynthia.

Jacques advanced several yards into the office. He paused at a shelf of religious artifacts and plucked a shofar from its perch. "You know I'm not a fan of Judaism—of any organized religion, for that matter—but even I'll admit that a well-crafted shofar is a magical instrument," he declared. "Secular composers are just starting to catch on. Did you know that Bernstein arranged a sonata entirely for rams' horns?"

Cynthia zipped shut her computer case and swung it over her shoulder.

"I'm actually on my way out," she said. "If you've come about the details for Sunday, I've already arranged to have you let in."

"Thank you. I really do appreciate it," said Jacques. "I know I promised you that I wouldn't ask for anything else," he continued. "But I'm desperate. I just heard the forecast—and it's supposed to pour all weekend."

A moment elapsed before Cynthia realized what the composer wanted. He'd set the shofar back on its perch and had turned to face her. His messianic expression sent a shiver up the back of her neck.

"No. Absolutely not," she answered. "Don't even ask."

"I'm not asking, I'm begging," said Jacques. "Some of these cellos are worth thousands of dollars. Nobody is going to risk opening them up in the rain . . . Try to understand where I'm coming from. God knows I've made a muddle of things over the years. I've squandered far too many opportunities—and I'm as aware of that as anybody. But I've dotted every I and crossed every T this time around. I've even convinced Pablo Casals' granddaughter to read an introductory poem. You can't imagine how much this performance means to me."

The composer's sincerity caught Cynthia off guard. She felt as though someone else had pulled a thread on her tallis.

"You were willing to let us rehearse here," Jacques persisted. "What's the difference?"

"It's not a personal choice," she said. "I have a duty to my congregation."

The composer held his palms out. "So why not invite them?"

"Because it's a sanctuary, not a concert hall," said Cynthia. "Your Cardinal Luciani isn't the only one who's entitled to maintain a modicum of holiness."

"That's not a reason," answered Jacques. "An excuse, maybe. But not a reason."

This accusation was too much for Cynthia. He was right—and she hated him for it.

"You want a reason? I'll give you a reason. Because I don't want to." And then she was sobbing, weeping as vulnerably as Rachel ever had for her children—and shame flooded her tear-caked cheeks.

Jacques attempted to wrap his arm around her quivering body, but she shook him off. "I don't know what got into me," she apologized, dabbing her eyeliner dry with a tissue. "I didn't mean that. Of course you can borrow the sanctuary on Sunday."

The composer gazed down at his sandals. "You don't have to do this," he said. "It's really not the end of the world. I'm sure something else will turn up."

"You're going to have your concert in the sanctuary. It's decided." Cynthia took a deep, determined breath. "If you don't, I'll never forgive myself."

She did not mention her breakdown to Jed. It was the first real secret she'd ever kept from him in their three years together, but she couldn't find the right moment to broach the subject. She certainly didn't dare discuss Jacques in front of her in-laws, and then she had her sermon to worry about, and Jed's Saturday afternoon was booked solid with his long-term psychoanalysis patients. By the time Sunday rolled around—a balmy June morning, glazed with cottony white clouds—the prospect of bringing up the encounter, two days after the fact, struck Cynthia as pointlessly incriminating. Not that she'd done anything wrong.

Strolling hand in hand with Jed toward the synagogue, along sycamore-shaded streets where raccoons foraged through trash cans and rambunctious children scampered between stoops, the rabbi assured herself that she had chosen wisely in turning the sanctuary over to Jacques' monolithic orchestra. This too, in its own peculiar way, was a mitzvah. She'd even announced the event during services the previous morning, as Jacques had suggested, although she doubted that many in her congregation of overbooked professionals and starter couples would actually come.

To Cynthia's husband, the prospect of four hundred cellos proved a source of considerable amusement. She'd hardly stepped out of the shower that morning when he'd asked, "What's that George Burns joke about why so many people take an instant dislike to the cello?" He had flashed her a look of intense satisfaction and answered, "It saves time." Over breakfast, he'd informed her that he too had played cello once—in a marching band. "You don't believe me," he insisted, beaming. "I used to borrow my grandmother's wheelchair and follow the bugle corps down Fifth Avenue." Yet by the time they arrived at the synagogue that afternoon, Jed sounded genuinely enthusiastic about the concert. "As someone who has no artistic talents myself," he observed, "the least I can do is live vicariously through others."

They climbed the steps of the synagogue on the heels of a teenage couple in shredded jeans and matching black T-shirts. Both shirts read "CELLO: BECAUSE SIZE MATTERS." The boy sported an earring shaped like a skull. In contrast, Cynthia was wearing her beige pantsuit and pumps. It had not crossed her mind to dress down.

Empty cello cases lined the vestibule opposite the coat room like coffins jettisoned haphazardly from a fleet of hearses.

"It's strange to go to shul as a spectator," Cynthia observed. "Honestly, it feels a bit like sneaking into your own funeral and sitting in the back row."

"Someone is in a light-hearted mood," said Jed.

He kissed the base of her wrist, apropos of nothing, and they seated themselves beneath the stained-glass portrait of Moses atop Mt. Sinai. The sanctuary was already bustling with cellists and their admirers. Musicians occupied the entire bema and fanned out through every spare aisle and alcove. Jacques had also commandeered the first ten rows of seats, covering them with plywood boards to create an elevated platform. He perched at the center of this makeshift stage, surrounded by several dozen junior cellists. The youngest was an Asian girl, a mere toddler, dwarfed by an instrument no taller than a fire hydrant. Jed noted that Jacques Krentz "looked like a brilliant composer," but at that moment, hemmed in by a brigade of worshipful children, her former lover reminded Cynthia of the Pied Piper of Hamelin.

Jacques raised his baton, and a hush descended on the sanctuary. The same resonant voice that had so recently begged the rabbi for folding chairs now introduced his "dear friend" Nikolai, a former student of the legendary Rostropovich. The granddaughter of Pablo Casals, Jacques reported, would be joining them only in spirit, as she had torn a ligament during a tennis match earlier that day. While Nikolai spoke of his mentor's love for grand and flamboyant musical gestures, a bearded man behind Cynthia snacked on pistachio nuts. Several of the leftover shells missed his discard bag and rolled beneath the rabbi's pew. For a moment, she also feared that she smelled marijuana, but she couldn't be certain.

"Only three hundred twenty-one cellos," whispered Jed. "I want my money back."

I want a lot of things right now, Cynthia thought. "Behave," she warned.

Jacques Krentz raised his baton a second time—and suddenly, eyes aglow and the veins in his neck throbbing, he did look like a brilliant composer. Cynthia closed her eyes. In the darkness, she had a clear vision of her ex-lover's impending triumph. At the end of the day, for all of her anxiety, the music would live up to the sanctity of the venue. She reached for her husband and clasped his fingers just as the cellists launched their opening salvo.

The first composition, an excerpt from a Liszt concerto, was what one might have expected from four hundred strangers thrown together for an afternoon medley: some excess vibrato, occasional grandstanding, and a few discordant notes. But it was on the next piece—the Bartok—that the performance descended into genuine cacophony. An old-timer in a tight-fitting tuxedo decided to play the entire work col legno, drawing the wooden side of his bow across the strings. One of the junior cellists burst out crying and charged from the stage. The performers atop the bema and those in the aisles battled over the tempo. With each passing moment, Jacques lost more control of his orchestra.

The Schoenberg symphony fared no better. But it was the John Cage finale, an avant-garde work that would have challenged audiences under the best of circumstances, that bordered on torture. Never had Cynthia heard such a jumble of unpleasant sounds—rendered much the worse by the all-too-audible exodus of spectators, many expressing their displeasure aloud as they stormed toward the exits. Several of the seasoned cellists gave up prematurely and silenced their instruments. As the noise approached a crescendo, Cynthia held her fingers to her ears and prayed for it to stop. Finally, tranquility came to the sanctuary, bringing relief to the few remaining onlookers. These survivors wore the dazed expressions of refugees. Nobody spoke. It was as though a millennial storm had ravaged the earth.

The musicians, sensing their defeat, departed quickly. Soon Jacques sat alone atop his improvised wooden deck. He buried his face in his hands. Cynthia felt an urge to approach him—to comfort him—but she lacked the words. Instead, she followed her husband into the vestibule, where the muted cellists were packing their instruments, and then out to the sidewalk.

"Well, that was something," an elderly man said to his wife.

"Wasn't it?" she answered, far too loud.

Jed wiped his glasses on his handkerchief. "I guess you won't be remembered as a historical footnote after all, honey."

He had meant nothing by this remark—nothing more than the obvious. That Jacques Krentz had once again managed a colossal failure. But for a fleeting instant, the rabbi hated her husband. At least her former lover could imagine an orchestra of four hundred cellos, a fantasy that was, by her husband's admission, beyond his own talents. At least Jacques still had dreams of grandeur. So who was Jed to judge? Cynthia spun toward her husband, intending to lash out at him in Jacques' defense—but she didn't. Her husband was smiling at her, his face open and innocent and loving. Not the look of a dreamer, by any stretch, but an ordinary kind of wonderful.

The rabbi rested her head on her husband's shoulder. Then she wrapped her arms around his chest as though accepting a blessing, grateful that she'd married a man who concealed his musical feats behind a shower curtain, and secure in the knowledge that life's great triumphs and calamities were safely behind her.

LIMERENCE

OF ALL THE SUBJECTS that my high school buddies squabbled about during the countless hours we wasted in Ted Zielberg's furnished basement—from the definitive meaning of *The Catcher in the Rye* to the amount of pine tar on George Brett's bat—the bulk of our attention focused on girls, and of all the girls we knew in Marston Moor, the one who preoccupied us most was Lena Limpetti. Because she lived across the street from me, and because our fathers carpooled together to Lutheran Hospital, where my dad practiced thoracic surgery and hers served as general counsel, the other guys considered me the resident expert on all things Lena, although the truth is that, long after I'd outgrown definitive meanings, professional baseball, and even my boyhood friends, Lena Limpetti remained for me a source of fascination and bewilderment. I am now a superior court judge here in Connecticut. I have presided over scores of marriages, dissolved billion-dollar corporations, and even sentenced one man to die. Nevertheless, the mere mention of Lena's name transforms me into the shy creature whose heart splintered every morning that I shared a school bus with her at the age of twelve.

Lena entered our lives in the middle of seventh grade—the same year I suffered through bar mitzvah lessons and my mother won election to the local school board. One weekend afternoon, I heard Lou Limpetti's gravelly voice in the foyer and then found myself summoned downstairs to meet his daughter, who'd moved east from California. And there she was: dark side-swept bangs, deep-set sapphire eyes, perfection. Lena's denim jacket hung open, a low-cut T-shirt embracing her already well-developed chest and exposing several inches of midriff. More bare flesh showed between her acid-wash jeans and her ankles, one of which was ringed by a glistening, stainless steel cuff.

"Jesse, this is Lena," said my father. "Mr. Limpetti's daughter."

"Hi, Jesse." Lena sounded confident and adult-like. "Good to meet you."

I froze. A formal introduction to someone my own age was entirely alien to my experience, and it didn't help that pretty girls intimidated the daylights out of me. We'd been studying Greek mythology that quarter in language arts, and the line that Miss Whitlock quoted relentlessly about Helen of Troy sprang into my thoughts: Was this the face that launched a thousand ships, and burnt the topless towers of Ilium? Somehow the "topless towers" drew my eyes downward to Lena's chest, and I felt blood surging into my cheeks. I must have looked in need of the Heimlich maneuver, and if I'd actually choked to death at that moment, I would have been grateful for the easy escape.

"Lena will be starting school with you on Monday," said my father. "Lou and I were hoping you would show her around, maybe introduce her to your friends . . ."

My father, Dr. Saul Neerman: well-intentioned and utterly oblivious. He thought so highly of me, his dutiful, straight-A+ son, that he genuinely believed a girl who looked and dressed like Lena Limpetti would want to play Ping-Pong and shoot darts with the likes of Ted Zielberg, Donald Schwartz, and beak-nosed Kenny Kalinovsky. "Sure," I agreed, my gaze focused on Lena's tiny, beaded moccasins, and I don't think I exhaled again until the storm door clanged shut behind our guests.

"Be kind to that girl," urged my father. "Her mother died. That's why she's moving here in the middle of the school year." Dad lit his churchwarden pipe—what he called his only indulgence, the one that would see him succumb to throat cancer at fifty-two—and the foyer filled with the sweet, fertile scent of his tobacco. "Besides, she's a cute one—and it's about time you had a girlfriend."

"Lena Limpetti isn't going to be my girlfriend," I snapped.

"Why not?"

"Jesus, Dad. It's just not going to happen."

"How will you know unless you try?" pressed my father. Dad subscribed to the surgeon's creed—sometimes right, always certain—and he parented as confidently as he operated. "Your mom was the best-looking coed in her class at Vassar, and a gentile with a rich father to boot, but did I let that stop me from sweeping her off her feet? Of course not." Dad squeezed my shoulder, as though to emphasize the muscle. "You're a handsome young man, Jesse. Don't sell yourself short."

I was not a particularly handsome young man, of course. And Marcy Doyle hadn't been the best-looking undergraduate at Vassar. But to my gloom-blind father, whose own father once vended cutlery from an Orchard Street pushcart and who would spend his final days on the ventilator planning for a lengthy retirement, all that stood between me and Lena's love—or any woman's affections— was the asking.

Because Lena's first day of classes fell on a Monday, and on Mondays my mother drove me to school at seven a.m. for my private cello lessons with Mr. Mobilio, I didn't encounter Lena again until Miss Whitlock's language-arts class. The girl's weekday outfit was, if anything, more provocative than her weekend wear: a sleeveless leather vest over a matching knee-length skirt. I feel the need to emphasize again that we were twelve years old—that for most of the girls in my classes, provocative attire meant sporting men's long johns instead of tights. When Miss Whitlock asked "our newcomer" if she had any questions ("You're our very own Odysseus, my dear"), Lena wondered whether she might address the elderly teacher by her first name, which prompted a response from Judith Whitlock so flustered and defensive that it still makes me cringe. During lunch, she ate with a trio of popular eighth-grade girls. One of Roger Sherman Middle School's star athletes swaggered up to her table and pressed a note into her palm; to my amazement, Lena winked at him and stuffed the note into her bra. I traced her every movement and committed it to memory until Kenny Kalinovsky warned me that my eyeballs might dislocate. Lena smiled at me several times that day, as though acknowledging our earlier meeting, but made no effort to chat.

I both longed for and dreaded the ride home, when I'd share forty-five minutes in an enclosed space with Lena, but to my surprise—and relief, and disappointment—our bus departed without her. That didn't prevent Ted Zielberg from scrawling "TZ & LL" inside a heart on the vinyl back of his seat, or Kenny from reminding him that Lena was "stratospherically" out of his league.

"A guy's allowed to dream," said Ted. "You're not jealous, are you?"

"Not of you," Kenny shot back. "I'm jealous of the dude who owns the keys to that cuff around her ankle."

The boys razzed each other until we reached Kenny's stop. I can't help wondering how many other boys, on other buses, were also staking a claim to Lena that afternoon. We were rounding the final curve on Laurendale Avenue when a motorcycle pulled up alongside us. The driver didn't wear a helmet. He was a lean, square-jawed fellow who could have been in high school or even college—although, as my dad might have said, he didn't look like the college type. His passenger, her arms wrapped around his waist, was unmistakably Lena.

She stood at the foot of her driveway, talking to the motorcyclist, while I climbed down the steps of the bus. My knapsack felt like a badge of shame. I was prepared to ignore her, but her companion drove off suddenly, leaving her alone.

"Hey, Jesse," she called out. "Can you do me a favor?"

I paused at a safe distance.

"If anybody asks," she said, "could you tell them I rode home with you on the bus?"

Until that afternoon, I'd lived in a world where a favor meant shoveling snow from a neighbor's driveway or jump-starting an acquaintance's car. I suppose I'd told my share of white lies before, but nobody had ever asked me to spread one.

"Was that your boyfriend?" I demanded.

"Larry?" Lena looked genuinely surprised—as though it had never entered her head that someone might think the good-looking older guy chauffeuring her home from school on his motorbike could be her boyfriend. "Lord, no. Larry's just someone I've been hanging out with," she explained. "I have a boyfriend back in California."

I suppose my face must have revealed my

disappointment, because Lena said, "We can hang out sometimes, too." And then she added, "Only don't tell anyone, okay?"

A wiser youth would have ended our encounter—and our relationship—then and there. All I managed to do was gripe, "You keep a lot of secrets, don't you?"

"I guess," Lena said. "I should probably be more honest . . . My dad doesn't know this, but I've been writing to my stepfather in jail."

When she mentioned her stepfather, it reminded me of her mother, and why she'd come to Marston Moor in the first place, and whatever anger I had felt about Lena's boyfriend melted instantly. I could not have imagined life without my own mother. Maybe if my mother had died, I thought, I'd also be mistrusting.

"I'm sorry about your mom," I said. "Really."

"Me, too."

"And I'm sorry your stepfather's in jail," I said. "Whatever he did, it must be awful to be in jail when you've just lost your wife."

Lena's gaze dropped to the asphalt, her opposite toe toying with the ankle cuff.

"Don't be too sorry for him," said Lena. "He killed her."

The Marston Moor where I grew up in the 1970s was one of those bedroom suburbs carved out of an old New England village. Second-generation Jewish professionals like my father grafted easily onto local stock, adding a dash of scrappy ambition and ethnic flavor to the pervasive atmosphere of Yankee propriety. All in all, it was a welcoming place, but a sterile one—a community that functioned primarily to get kids like me into places like Yale, which it ultimately did. Of my friends from that era, Ted Zielberg and Kenny Kalinovsky are both partners in white-shoe law firms, Harold Flinder serves as associate dean of a dental school in California, and Donald Schwartz—whose name you may recognize from the financial pages—has of late become one of the leading players in the commercial reinsurance business. Our parents were all liberal Republicans of the Rockefeller variety who went to synagogue twice each year to worship a benign, munificent God who cared passionately about SAT scores. We lived an hour by commuter train from Greenwich Village and twenty minutes' drive from the winding backstreets of working-class New Haven, but those neighborhoods, and their inhabitants, were as far away from us as the depths of the ocean.

Lena was everything that my friends and I were not: rebellious, volatile, sexy. Unabashedly directionless. Also damaged, possibly beyond repair, but in my school years I was oblivious to the depth of her wounds. Soon enough, we did hang out—on the rusting swing set in her father's backyard, then in the third-floor alcove where my mother had installed a pair of beanbag chairs—and I eventually assured myself that she'd been joking when she warned me not to tell anyone about us spending time together. Or, at least, half-joking. Our encounters arose at her initiative:

one day, Lena appeared at our door unexpectedly, asking to borrow my biology notes. A few afternoons later, she knocked without pretext and invited herself in to say hello— and after that, we rendezvoused every week or so, always on her schedule. Never did it cross my mind to invite her to Ted Zielberg's basement or to ask if I could join her and her clique of friends for their weekend parties or drinking excursions into New York City. Nor did we talk about the minor social triumphs and setbacks that defined our daily lives, and never once did she mention the countless guys, mostly older and rough edged, who paraded in and out of her house in weekly and monthly stints, nor did she reveal what had become of the boyfriend in California. Our friendship had tacit but well-defined boundaries.

What we did talk about was Lena's childhood. Not surprisingly, for a girl who'd lost her mother at the age of twelve, she spent most of our first months together telling stories of her mom's many exploits. What became clear to me, even if it wasn't as readily evident to Lena, was that all of her mother's adventures started and ended with liquor, or occasionally liquor and marijuana. The McKays had lived paycheck to paycheck, and sometimes hand to mouth, but with raucous pleasure—until the afternoon that a cocaine-revved Zane McKay drove his Oldsmobile into a bus of disabled children. When he awoke in intensive care three days later and discovered that his wife had died in the crash, he tried to hang himself with his hospital gown. "He loved my mother," said Lena. "Don't get me wrong. He's a stupid, lazy, alcoholic murderer, but he was crazy about that woman." Hearing Lena refer to her own mother as "that woman" was jarring to me, a reminder that a part of her remained perpetually detached from those around her. On another occasion Lena said matter-of-factly, "Her second husband used to beat the shit out of me and stick his hand down my pants. Zane just stole my cigarettes."

One night at the outset of ninth grade, in the middle of describing how her mother had been fired from a waitressing job for pouring creamer into the purse of a customer who'd under-tipped, Lena burst into tears. "I can't do it," she said between sobs. "I keep hoping if I describe her enough, she'll be real to you . . . but it doesn't work that way. If you haven't met someone, they can never be real to you."

I let her cry into my shoulder—the first time I'd ever touched her—and I held my breath, afraid that even the slightest motion on my part might cause her to remove her head. "I'm sorry," pleaded Lena. "I'm not usually like this with people, it's just that . . ."

"It's just what?"

"It's just that I know I can say anything to you, Jesse," she said, gently extracting herself from my embrace. "I guess I know you're going to like me no matter what I say, so I don't have to worry about what you think."

"Thanks," I said. "I guess."

"It's a compliment," said Lena. "It means I trust you."

I told myself this was a good sign. I knew deep down it was not.

೮

That same fall I started having Sunday suppers with the Limpettis. The idea of dining together as a family was a foreign custom to me. My mother's evenings were occupied with various civic duties, while my older sisters and I ate on our own routine, often the leftovers that my father brought back from his dinner talks for pharmaceutical companies. But Lou Limpetti had grown up in a traditional Italian family, the youngest of seven brothers, and now that his daughter was living under his roof, he was determined to reestablish some of the traditions of his own childhood for her benefit. I'll admit I was dumbfounded when Lena's dad first invited me to join them—but, in hindsight, I can see this was part of Lou's covert war against his daughter's defiance. I wasn't the only one clinging to a secret fantasy that Lena might someday marry a guy like me.

"He thinks you're a good influence on me," said Lena. "You're the only one of my guy friends he'll even let inside the house."

I knew very little about Lena's other guy friends. At first, the boys she hung out with were upperclassmen at Wolcott High—guys I recognized from the school cafeteria or had seen jogging around the track in their baseball uniforms. But by tenth grade, the men she dated were strangers: intimidating creatures whose long hair or steel-buckled boots shouted hell to the devil. No two of these men looked similar in any conventional sense, but each exuded his own distinctive brand of insolence. And they were men, not boys. One of them drove a low-riding Mustang with bumper stickers that read "DEATH MOBILE" and "ANTISOCIAL" emblazoned beside a skull and crossbones. Another sported a leather jacket whose back decal warned: "I KILL FOR MONEY."

Some weekend nights, if I was home alone, I'd peer through the upstairs blinds, hoping to catch a glimpse of Lena when her man du jour dropped her off at the foot of the driveway. I tortured myself watching her lock lips with a short, broad-shouldered guy with a shaved head, and a lanky, long-faced fellow who kept breaking their kiss to take drags on his cigarette. Then one spring night, a weather-beaten Plymouth stopped fifty yards up Laurendale Avenue, and as I watched, I realized that Lena and her date were engaged in more than kissing—an episode that brought a conclusive end to my years of petty voyeurism. I'd known all along, of course, that Lena was no vestal virgin. In fact, her lack of innocence was part of her appeal. Yet actually seeing her climb out the back door of a Plymouth made my insides churn.

The Sunday suppers at the Limpettis', in contrast, were tame affairs. If Lou knew that his daughter had a reputation across two states, he feigned the part of naïve parent to the hilt. As late as the fall of our senior year, he was encouraging his daughter to take part in extracurricular activities. "Don't they have a musical theater society or a choir?" he inquired one evening. "You've always had such a beautiful voice." Another day, he proposed that his daughter find a chapter of the Future Lawyers of America. "You don't have to become a lawyer, honey," he explained. "But it's a good credit to have on your record, in case you ever do decide to follow in your old man's footsteps."

Lena never declared any interest in singing or litigating or pursuing endeavors that might "pad her résumé"—to use Lou's expression—but she never resisted, either, as I did when my dad pressured me to ask out girls or to apply for summer internships at the White House and *The New York Times*, positions whose posted requirements included two years of college. When Lou urged, Lena merely smiled and allowed her father to have his say, and then she went about her business as though the topic had never been broached.

Our suppers stopped abruptly during March of our senior year when Lena's stepfather was released from prison. I found out when she borrowed a screwdriver to remove the stainless steel cuff from her ankle. Her skin, beneath the metal, had bleached to a sickly turquoise. "I feel so naked without it," she announced, then handed the metal ring to me. "A souvenir," she said. "You can boast to your friends that you possess Lena Limpetti's ankle cuff. That should get people talking." Moments like this, when Lena displayed an awareness of her image and her sexual power, challenged my fantasy that I might rescue her someday from her string of short-lived relationships.

Lena wanted to take off two weeks in the middle of the academic year to drive out to Fresno with a tattoo artist nicknamed the Ayatollah. She'd already been admitted to

NYU—largely because her father had joined the law faculty there to grease the admissions process—and she didn't see the point of treading water in high school when she could be seeing the world. Lou said no. Absolutely not. She went anyway.

"Do you know what she told me, Jesse?" her father asked.

I'd come over to dine that night at five o'clock to discover Lena's father alone, in his threadbare bathrobe, sipping a mug of hot cocoa at the kitchen table.

"She said I had two choices," explained Lou. "I could phone the police—and then they'd come after her, and probably arrest her boyfriend, but that would also likely mean the end of NYU and certainly of law school. Or I could call her in sick to school until she gets back." Lou cleaned his spectacles on his handkerchief. "I really should notify the police," he added. "Of course, she knows I won't dare."

"Lena's a smart girl," I said. "She'll be all right."

"I hope so," said Lou. "To tell you the truth, I'd feel much better if you were the one driving out there with her—and not that . . . that . . ." Lou Limpetti waved his hand, unable to find an appropriate description for the tattoo artist. "I know it's not my place, Jesse," he continued, "but I've always wondered why you . . . and Lena . . ." He paused, again at a loss for words. If we'd lived in the era of arranged marriages, I'd have had it made. As it was, Lou rose abruptly, as though he sensed he'd crossed a line. "Now that you're here," he declared, "I suppose you should stay for some risotto." And that was that.

Only that wasn't that. Once he'd planted the notion in my head that asking out Lena was more than a pipe dream, I wasn't able to concentrate on anything else. I couldn't even await her return from California. Instead, I penned a love letter, revealing the depth of my pent-up feelings and arguing a case for Jesse Neerman as a potential boyfriend. It was a masterpiece of a missive, if I do say so myself—six years of desire condensed into twelve handwritten pages. No legal brief I ever wrote in subsequent years was as passionate or logically airtight. Once I'd mailed it, of course, I second-guessed myself ruthlessly, irrationally convinced that my choice of phrasing might raise or lower my romantic prospects.

I knew Lena planned to return home for Easter, so I spent that weekend pacing the floorboards in the third-story alcove, periodically looking out the window for the Ayatollah's vintage Cadillac. Instead, Lena arrived by taxi after midnight on Saturday. (I later learned she'd had a falling out with the tattoo artist in Kansas City and had returned to Connecticut on a Greyhound bus.) She swung her duffel bag over her shoulder and disappeared into the house, and I didn't see or hear from her again until Monday at school.

School had always been a no man's land for Lena and me, a place where we acknowledged each other but rarely interacted. As the years passed and we were tracked into separate classes, our contact only decreased further. We had separate friends, divergent lives. So there was nothing unusual about her throwing me a smile in the cafeteria or waving to me in the gym corridor without striking up a conversation. Nothing, except that I'd sent her a letter pouring out my heart. Now I wondered: What if she hadn't received it? What if it had been damaged in transit or stolen by a mail-hoarding postal worker? Or intercepted by one of her countless male friends? The possibility that she had read the letter and was somehow still able to go about her daily routine was too much for my teenage soul to endure.

I skipped my French class that afternoon and sneaked down to the brook opposite the faculty parking lot, where Lena had a habit of sunning herself on the rocks. She was laying out with a pair of her friends, but when they saw me approaching, one of them whispered to her companion and they disappeared down the hillside, offering me friendly smiles as they passed. They knew.

Lena had unhooked her bikini to tan her shoulder blades; now she held her top to her chest with one hand while fastening the strap with the other.

"Hey," said Lena. "I missed you."

"Did you get my letter?" I asked.

She looked away. "Yes."

"And?"

"Thank you, Jesse. I wish I could write like that."

"That's all?"

"You're so sweet . . . and . . ."

"And what?"

I could hear a chord of desperation in my voice, even hostility. In the stream, a Canada goose led a procession of goslings in search of prey.

Lena said, "What else do you want me to say?"

"That you feel the same way? Or at least that you'll try?"

Lena shook her head, and I was surprised to see that she was close to tears. "Please don't ruin things," she said softly. "Everything else is already falling apart. I know I should be grateful to you for writing me such a beautiful letter, but I can't do that right now. I just can't."

I clung to the temporality of her rejection. Right now, she'd said.

"It's okay," I said. "We don't have to talk about that now. Or ever, if you don't want to." I slid down beside her on the sunbaked slab of granite. "How was California?" I asked, hoping to change the subject. "How was your stepfather?"

She clutched her arms over her chest, and her entire body started to quiver.

"He hanged himself," she said. "The night before we got there."

That afternoon could have been a moment that brought Lena and me closer together, but instead it was the point of no return on the path that would lead us apart. Shortly afterward, I received my acceptance letter from Yale, which I'd chosen over Columbia because it was coed, and my life was consumed with purchasing textbooks and triaging my belongings so my mother could transform my childhood bedroom into a home office. To my surprise, I proved far more successful with women in New Haven than I had in Marston Moor—and one night, during the spring of my sophomore year, I went on a double date with Harold Flinder, who'd also chosen Yale over Columbia, and I met Sheila. We've been together ever since—twenty-eight years, next June—and she's inherited my mother's position on the Marston Moor School Board and her chairmanship of our local League of Women Voters chapter. I suppose a psychiatrist might find these facts revealing, or even alarming, but I've never had call to visit a psychiatrist.

Lena and I exchanged letters during our first year away from home. I tried to render mine as compelling as circumstances would allow, storing up exciting anecdotes and subjecting them to the occasional embellishment, but I imagine my weekly ramblings proved a tedious read. I'd discovered ancient history that autumn—not Judith Whitlock's mythical Troy, but the actual derring-do of Xenophon and Thucydides—and I filled pages of onion skin paper comparing my own life to those of Spartan generals and Persian princes. I suspect Lena devoted far less thought to her half of our correspondence, which contained an endless series of references to people I'd never met and musicians I'd never heard of and nightclubs that would likely have kept me waiting at the door until all the VIPs had departed. And then her letters stopped entirely. About six months afterward, I received a phone call from Lena—collect, from a pay telephone—telling me she was planning to pass through New Haven en route to a music festival in Halifax and asking if she could crash in my dormitory room for the night. I agreed, of course—but she never showed up.

By then, I'd learned from my father that she'd given up on NYU entirely and was supporting herself singing at private parties. "If you believe that, I'll sell you a bridge over the East River," added my dad. "Lou can call it singing, if he has to, but I'd guess that girl is doing a lot more than crooning show tunes for her keep, if you want my opinion."

"I don't want your opinion."

"Touchy, touchy," said my father, his voice already raspy from the tumor. "I know you always had a soft spot for the girl, Jesse, but she was a bad apple." Dad had given up tobacco but not the pipe itself, and he gripped the narrow stem between his teeth. "We should all be thankful you left her alone. Can you imagine what life would be like married to a woman like her?" He coughed sharply, then cocked his head and said something I'll never forget. "From the start, you could tell she was one of those girls who believe 'pretty' is going to take them further than it actually will." My father beamed at me, proud of his armchair analysis. He had spoken of Lena in the past tense, and somehow that seemed fitting, as though she had already evaporated into memory.

Years passed. We buried my father after a small graveside service, followed by a larger tribute at the synagogue several months later. Lou Limpetti did not attend the memorial, but he sent my mother a heartfelt card. I subsequently heard from my mother that he'd remarried and moved to a planned community in the Hudson Valley.

My parents had once been the youngest couple on our block. Now my mother was a woman of a certain age, surrounded by starter families. Sheila and I made a point of visiting her every other weekend, bringing the girls to spend time with their grandmother, but after my father's death I never felt fully at home again on Laurendale Avenue. I looked forward to the day when Mom would downsize to an apartment in Stamford or Bridgeport, when I could put behind me forever my weekend nights in Ted Zielberg's drafty basement and the torture of my morning bus rides alongside Lena Limpetti. But my mother could no more imagine life outside Marston Moor—where she ran the historical society and kept minutes for the Town and Village Club—than I could envision life without her. So after the upheaval of my father's death, and marriage, and children, our lives flat lined comfortably to the routine that had always been written into the script, even if I hadn't always realized it.

It was toward the end of this period of calm and contentment—shortly before my mother's first hip fracture, and while the winds of female adolescence remained at bay—that Lou Limpetti telephoned me in my chambers. He still sounded as though he were gargling pebbles, and I recognized his voice instantly. My first thought, as he asked after my welfare, was that Lena was dead. But when he congratulated me on my recent appointment to the bench, it struck me that she might be in legal trouble.

"I'm sure your mother is mighty proud of you," said Lou. "I always thought the world of you myself. You were always looking out for Lena, and I'm grateful for that. Truly I am."

"Thank you," I said. "It means a lot."

Lou had called in the middle of a mediation session. I stepped into the restroom with the telephone receiver and pulled the door shut behind me, leaving the parties and their attorneys to wait in awkward silence for my return.

"I hope you'll forgive me for calling out of the blue like this," Lou continued. "But I hear that you're a father now, so I hope you can understand. Honestly, I didn't know where else to turn."

I put off the trip to Greenwich Village until the weekend. When Saturday rolled around, I convinced myself that another week or two wouldn't make any difference. After all, Lena hadn't spoken to her father in more than a year. Besides, I assured myself, I didn't have any leverage with Lena. I was just the vestige of an unpopular kid who'd had a crush on her in high school. If she paid my memory any heed at all, I was assuredly an afterthought—possibly even a nuisance. And it was knowing how little I mattered to Lena that kept me from boarding the train in Marston Corners for the hour-long trip into the city.

Sheila, of all people, finally pushed me to act.

"Imagine if one of the girls wasn't speaking to us," she said, massaging my shoulders. "How would you feel about a few weeks' delay then?"

I couldn't have endured a day, let alone a year, without my daughters.

"You won't mind?" I asked—hoping, I suppose, that

she might.

"Why should I mind? You're a grown adult, Jesse Neerman. If you want to run off with an old flame, that's between you and her. But if you're not coming home, have the decency to call so I know not to save your dinner."

I squeezed Sheila's hand. "It would serve you right if I did run off."

"I'll take my chances, your honor," she said, rolling her eyes. "But please don't forget your umbrella on the train again. Umbrellas don't grow on trees."

Three hours later, I was standing outside the alternative crafts and jewelry shop where Lena worked behind the counter, peering through the rain-dappled windows. Inside, the shop smelled pungently of incense, but beneath that hung the scent of stale tobacco—and possibly marijuana. I'd worn a fisherman's knit sweater and slacks, wishing to appear casual, but I stood out abysmally among the young, female clientele. At the door, I squeezed past a chubby teenage girl with chains connecting her earlobes to her septum.

"Can I help you?" asked the salesclerk.

Lena's deep-set sapphire eyes remained as gripping as ever, but she'd framed them with jet-black liner. The rest of her face had the weary look of someone for whom every social action was a struggle. Not that she wasn't still beautiful—she remained stunning, certainly for a woman past forty—but now a careful observer could foresee the day when she would be "beautiful once," which is the cruelest of life's compliments. Yet all of my old feelings surged back without warning, as though I'd always harbored the hope that Lena might yet fall for me, someday, somehow, a dream preserved like a firefly in a jar. I must have stared at Lena too long, because a vague irritation crossed her lips.

"Is something wrong?" she demanded.

"Lena," I said. "It's really you."

That was enough to flood her with recognition. She hugged me immediately, wrapping her slender arms around my chest, but it was the careless embrace of someone willing to hug almost anybody. "Jesus, Jesse," she said. "I could kick myself for not recognizing you."

"It's been a long time," I said.

"Too long," she answered. She took me by the hand and led me behind the counter, toward a tiny office that doubled as a lounge. On the way, she asked the teenager with the facial chains to cover the cash register for her.

"What in the world are you doing here?" Lena demanded. She released my hands and said, "Please don't tell me my father sent you." Then her expression hardened. "He did, didn't he?"

I said nothing. Under the incandescent light of the cluttered office, Lena's makeup proved less effective at concealing her age.

"I don't owe him anything," said Lena. All the joy had melted from her voice, replaced by a raw anger that was unfamiliar to me. "I don't owe anybody anything. He can take his Sunday suppers, and his musical theater society, and his goddamn NYU education, and he can flush it all down the toilet." Lena grabbed a pillow off the sofa and pounded it with her fist. "And who do you think you are coming down here like his fucking ambassador? Jesus Christ! Do you think you're the only guy who ever wrote me a love letter? If I had a dollar for every guy who wrote me a letter I didn't want, I'd never have to work again." Then Lena started crying, and despite her invective I held her head against my sweater until her tears ran dry.

"I didn't mean that," she said. "Not the way it sounded."

"It's all right," I soothed her. "I know."

We were seated on the sofa, opposite a horizontal mirror with a baroque frame, and in the reflection I saw a well-dressed, not unhandsome father of three comforting a deeply vulnerable woman who was not his wife. Anyone watching us, even for a brief moment, would have realized that I was the one who got away, not Lena—anyone but the two of us, that is—so I stood up quickly and glanced pointedly at my watch. "I can't stay," I apologized, surprising myself as much as her. "It was great to see you," I added, "but I really have to get back to Connecticut." Lena reached for my hand, but I eluded her and retreated quickly through the shop and then out onto the sidewalk. Outside, the streets of the West Village were all drizzle and mist. I had an hour to kill before my train departed, so I purchased a spare umbrella to replace the one I had lost the previous week. Then I walked north toward Grand Central Station, an umbrella in each hand, wishing that Lena Limpetti would come chasing after me through the rain.

EINSTEIN'S BEACH HOUSE

FROM 1946 UNTIL HIS DEATH in 1955, during his final years at Princeton, Albert Einstein spent his summers at 2647 South Ocean Avenue in Hager's Head, New Jersey. I know the precise location because in 1978, long after the physicist's beach house had been demolished for condominiums, the American Automobile Association's state guidebook listed the address as 2467 South Ocean Avenue—which happened to be the street number of an eleven-year-old girl named Natalie Scragg who planned on becoming the nation's first female astronaut, as well as her six-year-old sister, Nadine, and her financially strapped parents, Bryce and Delia, who made ends meet each year by renting out the bottom floor of the residence from May to September. And that eleven-year-old girl happened to be me. I never found out whether

AAA's mistake had merely been typographical or the book's authors genuinely believed that Professor Einstein had relaxed in our family's dilapidated bungalow, but—whatever the cause—the error brought curious tourists to our door that summer by the carload.

We were enjoying the breeze on the wraparound porch one June morning when the first batch arrived: two potbellied men on the far side of fifty, obviously brothers, possibly even twins, driving a battered Oldsmobile with Connecticut plates. One wore a vintage Brooklyn Dodgers cap; the other sported a comb-over. The duo stood at the curb, eyes shifting from house to guidebook to house again, until the bare-headed brother called out, "We're looking for the Einstein cottage."

"Well," Mama called back, "you've come to the wrong place."

The men showed my mother the address in their guidebook; she had them back inside their vehicle thirty seconds later. My father, engrossed in the blueprints for his latest invention, didn't even glance up until they'd departed.

"What a pain in the ass," said Mama. "Like Einstein would ever live in this dump. Bryce, you're going to have to put up a sign."

"I've got a better idea," said my father.

Mama rolled her eyes. "Aren't you too old for 'better ideas'?"

My father had been laid off from the Linguistics Division at Bell Labs that winter over what he described as "stylistic differences" with his bosses. What they'd actually disagreed about was the marketability of my father's latest gizmo: a device that supposedly translated "cat" and "dog" into human. Ever since, we'd been living off the proceeds of Mama's voice lessons while my father filed patents and tape-recorded house pets.

"Next time, we'll give them a tour," said my father. "For twenty-five dollars."

"A tour of what?" asked Mama.

"Of what they want. Einstein's beach house."

I'd been listening to this exchange while I completed my fractions homework.

"Did Einstein really live here?" I asked.

My mother said no and my father said yes simultaneously.

"Einstein did not live here, Nat," Mama said firmly.

"They why did Papa say he did?" I asked.

"Because sometimes your father is too clever for his own good."

&

The two-story wood-frame bungalow at 2647 South Ocean Avenue had served my father's family for four generations. Originally, "The Cottage" had been a "beach house"—a fashionable summer address for my great-grandparents—but after the stock market crash of '29 forced my father's grandfather from his Washington Square townhouse, the Scraggs took refuge on the Jersey Shore, and we'd been muddling along there ever since. I recently read in a magazine that, on average, it takes four generations to squander a large fortune; if that's true, our family was People's Exhibit A. My father completed our social descent when he eloped with Mama, a Jewish-atheist folk singer who'd dropped out of NYU to follow Jefferson Airplane on its West Coast tour. They'd met at Grand Central Station, on New Year's Day, 1968, after my father absentmindedly wandered into the ladies' restroom by mistake.

My parents had been a bad match from the get-go. Even at the age of eleven, I could sense this to be the case—and sometimes, while they were bickering, I wondered why they didn't just get divorced. The fundamental difference between them was that, for all her superficial radicalism and musical aspirations, Mama could be ruthlessly practical when the occasion demanded it. But my father, rest his soul, teared up at Disney movies and never embraced a pipe dream that didn't end in a pot of gold and a Nobel Prize. So the two of them argued about whether to withhold the tenant's security deposit over a chipped mirror, when to force Grandpa Byron into a nursing home, and even how much to tip the postman at Christmas. No decision was too trivial for a spat. At first, the Einstein error simply gave them one more issue to slam doors about.

"Bryce! Bry-yce!" shouted my mother the next morning, waking every living creature within a fifty-yard radius, and possibly some dead ones, too. Usually she kept her voice down during the summer months so as not to disturb the tenants, but Dr. Arcaya and his wife—the

Spanish couple who'd leased the place that year—had been called home abruptly for a funeral. Mama took advantage of their absence to exercise her vocal cords. I pulled my pillow over my ears, but it proved futile. Since we'd all relocated upstairs to accommodate the Spaniards, an annual ritual, even whispers resounded through the musty, cedar-paneled corridors like thunder. "Bryce! What in God's name is that?"

"Oh, that," replied my father, his voice soft and level. "That's a pig fetus in a jar. It was one of Einstein's prized specimens."

"Like hell it was!"

"It's the best I could do on short notice. There's a guy at Bell who owns a whole collection—human ones, too—but all he would lend me was a pig."

I glanced across our bedroom at Nadine. My sister was sitting up on the folding cot, hugging Mister Neck, her stuffed giraffe, to her chest. I longed to whisper reassurances to her, but I didn't want Mama to hear that we were awake.

"What is wrong with you, Bryce?" demanded Mama. "Do you realize how ridiculous you sound? And Einstein wasn't even a biologist. He was a physicist. What on earth would he want with a dead pig?"

"Point taken," agreed my father. "I know it's not ideal. But biological artifacts are easier to come by than physics artifacts . . . I can't exactly build a plutonium reactor in the cellar."

"I wouldn't put it past you."

"You've got to have faith in me on this one, Delia,"

said my father. "I did manage to set up a portable chalkboard in the kitchen. I'm going to cover it with equations copied from Uncle Bernard's old math textbooks and tell them it's Einstein's handwriting. We're charging only twenty-five dollars a head. They can't expect too much."

"We're not charging anything," snapped Mama. "You're charging twenty-five dollars. I'm minding my own damn business."

Then the door to the master bedroom crashed against its wooden frame—the reverberations rippling through the house like an earthquake—and we knew their conversation had ended.

"It will be okay," I promised Nadine. "Now get dressed, and I'll make you Jell-O for breakfast. Mister Neck can have some, too."

Nadine eyed me warily, tweezing her lower lip between her teeth, and asked, "Nat, what's a fetus?"

Mama remained true to her word. When my father returned home from the municipal library that afternoon with a stack of physics texts and Einstein biographies, from which he insisted upon reading aloud over dinner, she carried her meal out onto the veranda. When he nailed a sign above the bay windows announcing "EINSTEIN'S SUMMER RESIDENCE, GUIDED TOURS $25", I had to hold the base of the stepladder steady for him because Mama adamantly refused to assist. And when a jalopy full of female graduate students from Cornell arrived the next day, asking where they could purchase tickets for the "Einstein Museum," Mama shrugged her shoulders mutely like a benighted idiot and flipped open a magazine. "Your mother will be singing a different tune," chimed my father, "when it comes time to spend the money."

That first guided tour got off to a shaky start. Two of the graduate students were pursuing engineering degrees, and another was a chemist, and all five of the women knew far more about Albert Einstein, science, and even basic geography than my father did. When he explained that the physicist had chosen the Jersey Shore because it reminded him of his boyhood summers swimming off Rügen Island in the North Sea—a tidbit Papa had picked up from his reading—one of the graduate students informed him that the Prussian resort sat on the Baltic. "And I thought Einstein didn't know how to swim," interjected her companion. "Wasn't his wife always worried that he'd fall out of their sailboat?"

"I meant swimming metaphorically," replied my father. "I suppose I should have said wading to be thoroughly accurate." He whistled in contrived amazement. "I can't get anything past you ladies, can I?"

Papa led the coeds onto the third-story balcony where his version of Einstein once had enjoyed stargazing.

"Did you buy the house from him?" asked the first girl.

The girl was a tall, gangly creature with glasses, sporting a huge, floppy-brimmed straw hat à la Brigitte

Bardot. She was apparently writing her dissertation on Einstein's views regarding reincarnation. I immediately registered that she wasn't pretty.

"Oh, no. I'm not that old." Papa led the women down the stairs again, into the cozy corner bedroom—my bedroom—where he revealed Enrico Fermi had slept when he'd visited. "I bought this place from his niece many years after he died."

"I didn't realize he even had a niece," observed the girl in the straw hat. "I didn't think his sister, Maja, had any children."

"I could have sworn that woman said she was a niece." My father never lost his composure or his smile. "But maybe she said cousin. It was eons ago . . . What really matters is that I have the deed in my safe deposit box."

If the girls departed harboring suspicions, at least they didn't demand their twenty-five dollars back. Later that afternoon, my father repeated his performance—with fewer challenges—for two retired couples driving from Maine to Florida and a college professor visiting from Antwerp. At the end of the day, the take was $275. That was as much as Mama usually earned in a week of singing lessons—a fact that wasn't lost on yours truly, especially when Papa gave Nadine and me five dollars and sent us down to Robustelli's for milk shakes.

The next day we had three visitors—Rutgers undergrads—and the day after that, a Saturday, we lured in a whopping fourteen tourists. It helped that we were one of the few attractions listed in the AAA guide between Belmar and Atlantic City. Twenty-five dollars was an exorbitant admission fee, especially for 1978, but after a long drive down the coast, nobody wanted to walk away empty-handed. My father served complimentary root beer—which he claimed had been Einstein's favorite soft drink—to make his victims feel that they'd received their money's worth. Later he printed up T-shirts for three dollars each and sold them at the end of the tour for eight. By the time Dr. Arcaya returned from Barcelona, fifteen days later, my father's sightseeing enterprise was averaging $2,200 a week.

"What is this all about?" inquired Dr. Arcaya.

He was an elderly veterinarian and amateur ornithologist who'd come to New Jersey to research shorebirds, and the truth was that the man's face had grown to resemble the sandpipers and plover he studied. His wife, whose younger sister had died in a bus accident, was staying in Europe for another few weeks.

"I have good news, and I have bad news," explained my father. "The bad news is that this place might not be as quiet as I promised. Albert Einstein used to live here, you know, and one of the touring associations has gotten wind of it. Can't be helped." He rested his palm on the hunch of the Spaniard's stooped back, as though they were intimate friends. "The good news is that—in consideration of the inconvenience—I'm willing to cut fifty dollars a month from your rent. Pretty good deal, no?"

"I don't need a good deal," grumbled Dr. Arcaya. "I need peace and quiet."

"I knew you'd understand," continued my father,

utterly ignoring the old man's complaint. "You're a good sport. And like I said, it can't be helped."

Papa proved equally glib with Mrs. Ingersoll, a rotund, would-be cabaret sensation who took biweekly lessons from Mama during which the woman demonstrated an uncanny knack for butchering an extraordinary repertoire of music: one afternoon she'd botch the lyrics to "I Could Have Danced All Night," and the following week she'd miss every high note in "I'm in Love with a Wonderful Guy." Mrs. Ingersoll's husband apparently volunteered as the Hager's Head Village Historian—the couple had lived in the hamlet since 1938—and they both recalled Professor Einstein staying at a bungalow far closer to town. The woman told my father as much after one of her voice lessons.

"We'd bump into Mr. Einstein strolling on the beach quite often," said Mrs. Ingersoll. "Down by Cobb's Cove. I distinctly remember him telling us that he didn't own an automobile—that he didn't even know how to drive. And don't you tell me otherwise; I have the memory of an elephant. Now wouldn't you think it rather strange for Mr. Einstein to take the bus out beyond Cobb's Cove just to stroll along the beach, when he had a beach in his own backyard?"

My father held his palms skyward in a gesture of bewilderment. "He was a genius, Mrs. Ingersoll. There's no explaining genius," Papa replied. "And if you'll forgive me for saying so, your voice is growing more beautiful by the week. I'm honestly expecting to see you on Broadway one of these days."

The obese woman beamed. "Don't be foolish. At my age, I'm lucky that they'll let me inside the theater to watch." Yet Papa's charm had worked its magic: soon enough, Charlie Ingersoll was sending his own houseguests to tour the site.

After Mrs. Ingersoll had waddled down to her Cadillac, Mama joined my father on the veranda. It was early evening: the sun nipped the western hills, and the air smelled pungently of brine and pine needles. School was already out for the summer by then, so I'd spent the afternoon drafting lunar modules on graph paper. Nadine hid under the deck, teaching Mister Neck about bomb shelters. She was in her nuclear-war phase. To my surprise, Mama snuck up behind my father and wrapped her arms around his chest.

"I've got to hand it to you, Bryce Scragg," she said. "Do you realize we can actually pay the property taxes on time this year?"

My father spun to face her. "So you admit it was a better idea?"

"Better. Comparatively," Mama conceded, but she wore a broad grin. "It's all relative. Just don't start translating your tours into cat-speak or dog-lish."

Then they kissed. It was the first time I'd seen my parents kissing—or kissing passionately, at least, as opposed to mere pecks on the lips.

"If that's what better means," said Papa, coming up for air, "I'll be more than glad to settle for better."

That was the happiest I can ever remember them together—before or since. Two days later, Einstein's niece appeared on the doorstep.

My parents had just settled down to breakfast that morning when a metallic clank at the door set the basset hounds yelping. Whoever had called on us was rapping the ornamental gargoyle knocker rather than ringing the bell. My father, suspecting an early customer, went downstairs to welcome our guest. I followed. It was Bastille Day, I recall vividly, because Mama had placed a long-distance telephone call that morning—the only international call she made each year—to her childhood friend in Marseilles.

My father opened the door to a small, sharp-featured woman of about seventy. She wore a turquoise jacket, a matching ankle-length skirt, and a pillbox hat: The outfit made her look like the private secretary of a 1950s diplomat. In one gloved hand, she carried a clutch purse; the other rested on a cane. Pinned beside her lapel was a gemstone brooch shaped like a serpent. All in all, our visitor conveyed an aura of solemnity—even menace. Nothing about her suggested that she'd come for a guided walking tour of Albert Einstein's beach house.

"May I help you?" inquired my father.

"That depends," she answered—with an accent that I'd later discover to be Swiss. "I'm looking for Bryce Scragg."

"Then you've come to the right place. I'm Bryce

Scragg."

My father extended his hand. She did not shake it.

"And you are?" asked my father.

"Dora Winterer," said our guest.

Her very name launched a chill through my bones. I inched backward toward the staircase.

"You'll invite me inside, Mr. Scragg," Miss Winterer said—half-question, half-demand. "I'm not in the habit of discussing my private business en plein air."

"I didn't know we were discussing private business," Papa said defensively.

"There's a lot you don't know, Mr. Scragg."

I was accustomed to Mama shouting at my father, but that was far less upsetting that this woman's blunt contempt. Her attitude made my head warm with anger. Miss Winterer followed Papa up to the second-story landing, and if I could have done so with impunity, I would have gladly shoved her back down the steps. We crossed through the dining room en route toward the rear of the house, and my father said to Mama, "This lady would like a private word with me. I'm going to take her to the study."

"Is this your wife, Mr. Scragg?" asked Miss Winterer.

Mama looked up from her eggs. "I'm Mrs. Scragg," she said.

"In that case," said our visitor, "I think you'll want to join us."

A frown panned across my mother's face: she wasn't accustomed to being spoken to in Miss Winterer's tone—and she clearly resented it. Nevertheless, she stepped ahead of the old woman and vanished into the designated room.

My father kneeled down to meet my gaze at eye level. "Here's ten dollars," he said. "Go find your sister and walk her over to Robustelli's. Hold her hand while you cross the avenue and make sure she gets her fair share."

I didn't do anything of the sort, of course. I waited until they'd left the dining room, then descended the staircase with heavy footsteps and climbed back up on tiptoes. Fortunately, they'd left the door to the study slightly ajar. With my body pressed up against the entrance to the linen closet, I could see Miss Winterer ensconced on the sofa and my parents seated nearby in the matching armchairs. The old lady's mottled skin looked less than human under the white morning light.

"You've furnished it differently, that's for certain," declared Miss Winterer, surveying the room. "But it's more or less as I remember it."

"You've been here before?" asked Mama.

"Many years ago," answered Miss Winterer. "I used to visit my uncle."

"Your uncle lived here?" pressed Mama.

"Indeed, he did," said Miss Winterer. "But you already know that."

A silence enveloped the study. The old lady sat rigid as a corpse, her gloved hands folded in her lap.

"I'm not sure I understand," ventured my father.

"What is there to understand?" Miss Winterer wore a fierce expression. "My uncle was Albert Einstein."

My parents exchanged concerned looks.

"There must be a misunderstanding," said Mama. "Your uncle didn't actually live here. That's just a misprint in a tour book."

"Nonsense. Of course Uncle lived here," Miss Winterer shot back. "Don't think I'm a fool, Mrs. Scragg. I may be many things, but a fool is not one of them."

"Nobody's saying you're a fool—"

"Then what precisely are you saying, Mrs. Scragg? You may have hoodwinked me once, but you're not going to do it again."

My father crossed his legs. He looked uncharacteristically nervous. "I don't follow," he said.

"I hadn't realized Uncle still owned this place when he passed on . . . I suppose I just assumed he'd sold it long before that. I was living abroad at the time, you understand—I much prefer the climate on the Continent— and some matters fell through the proverbial cracks. Uncle's lawyers were a dastardly, incompetent lot. But when that girl telephoned me last week with all those questions about the house, I decided to dig to the bottom of this matter, as you say."

"What girl?"

"Some girl. I don't know her name—and it doesn't matter." Miss Winterer waved her hand in indifference and then leaned forward as though she might spit venom. "She was from Cornell, if that helps. Found my name in the phone directory. She told me she toured the premises a few weeks ago and you informed her that you'd bought this house from me. Is that so?"

"I must have misspoken," said my father, his voice rising. "The truth is that your uncle never lived here. In all likelihood, ma'am, he never even set foot in this place. My family has owned this house for generations. Since the turn of the century."

Miss Winterer laughed—a short, jagged chortle. "Really? Do you have a deed?"

My father glanced at Mama and then refocused on Miss Winterer. "I have it somewhere," he said. "I'm sure I do."

"I highly doubt that, Mr. Scragg," retorted the old woman. "Like I told you, I'm not a fool. Or senile. Not yet, at least. And I remember this house." She enunciated each syllable—as though choosing every word with the precision of a sniper. "Moreover, I do have a deed. Dated July 5, 1946, from Mr. Henry Sucram to Dr. Albert Einstein. And I also have a last will and testament, bequeathing all of the real and personal property of Dr. Albert Einstein, except as noted elsewhere, to his only niece, Miss Dora Winterer of Zurich, Switzerland." The elderly woman boosted herself to her feet without warning, resting both palms atop her walking stick. "Now if you'll excuse me, Mr. Scragg, Mrs. Scragg. I think we're through here. My attorneys will take care of the rest."

Mama stepped between Miss Winterer and the door. "Okay, let's say you have a deed. So what do you want from us?"

Now it was Miss Winterer who appeared genuinely surprised: her penciled eyebrows lifted in wonder. "I thought that was obvious," she said. "I want Uncle's house back." She sidestepped Mama and added: "I'm a reasonable woman, so I'll give you until the first of the month to vacate the premises. Then I'll have to send for the county marshal."

Miss Winterer strode into the hallway before I had an opportunity to retreat.

"Young lady," she said to me, her voice whetted with malice, "in the future, I'll advise you not to get caught eavesdropping. It's unbecoming."

And then the turquoise square of her hat disappeared down the stairs.

&

What my father actually found in his safe-deposit box was an architect's blueprint of "The Cottage" from when Grandpa Byron had expanded the kitchen and added on a pair of upstairs bedrooms for his teenage daughter. Papa also returned with a stack of bankbooks to long-closed accounts, stock certificates from defunct corporations, and a handwritten draft of Great-grandpa Benedict's unfinished memoir. He failed to bring home any evidence that he owned the house. The following morning, his visit to the village recorder's office proved even less promising: listed under 2467 South Ocean Avenue, the most recent transfer of title named the seller as Henry L. Sucram and the buyer as Albert Einstein. My father suspected that a subsequent page might have been torn from the digest—but as Mama pointed out, that still wouldn't have explained how either Sucram or Einstein came to claim a property in 1946 that my great-grandfather had purchased during the 1890s. (Under 2647, where Einstein had actually summered, the register made no mention of the physicist.) When my father hired a Trenton lawyer to investigate Miss Winterer's claim, the attorney phoned him back to reject the case within twenty-four hours. I listened in from the extension in the upstairs parlor.

"I hate to turn down business," the lawyer informed Papa, "but whoever sold you that place really pulled a number on you. Not only did title pass to Einstein in 1946, but the probate court awarded the property to his heirs in 1955. You can't even file an adverse possession claim—the current owners have thirty years to assert their rights, and it's only year twenty-three . . . Now if you'd like to sue the bastard who sold you the place, that's a horse of a very different color."

"But I didn't buy the place from anyone, goddammit," my father shouted as soon as he'd hung up the receiver. "How am I supposed to sue someone who doesn't exist?"

Papa's body followed his voice into the parlor. "Tell me something, Natalie, do I look crazy to you? Do you think your father's gone off the deep end?"

I didn't know how to answer that question, so I said nothing.

"Don't let anyone ever tell you that your old man is crazy, Nat," he said. "That's one of the only things I'll ask of you after I'm gone. If anybody ever says your old man went soft in the head, you set them straight. Or sock 'em in the kisser." He cupped his fist in his palm. "You do that and you'll make your old man proud."

My parents had reverted to squabbling while Miss Winterer's seat in the study was still warm, but it took a week of Mama's snide remarks and oblique criticism before their tepid skirmishes boiled over into an outright conflagration. By then, my father had exhausted every legal and tactical angle in his dispute with Einstein's niece, so he'd spent the last few days pacing himself toward exhaustion on the veranda. But that night was Nadine's seventh birthday—July 21, 1978—and both of my parents were striving for a festive mood on her account. My father had even poured himself a snifter of brandy to facilitate his good cheer.

The evening started off well enough: Mama served a fudge-frosted cake, and my sister made her wishes. Unfortunately, the assortment of toys and dollhouse accessories that my mother had gift-wrapped for the occasion did not include the only present that Nadine had been insisting she wanted all month: a Geiger counter. When her desire went unfulfilled, my sister pounded her fists on her place mat and ran bawling from the table.

"Why don't we just get it for her?" asked my father. "How much do you think one costs?"

Mama stopped clearing the cake plates. "Don't be absurd. We're not getting a seven-year-old girl a Geiger counter. Besides, we're in no position to be throwing money around. We could be homeless in ten days."

"What's that supposed to mean?"

"You know exactly what that means," said Mama. "I'm going to call tomorrow morning about putting the furniture into storage. We can stay with my sister, if we have to, until we find a rental."

"So you're taking her side!"

"I'm not taking anybody's side, Bryce. I'm taking reality's side." Mama deposited the plates in the sink and turned on the faucet. "And the reality is that I don't want my daughters living on the street."

"It won't come to that."

"No, it won't. That's why I'm arranging a backup plan."

Mama continued washing dishes. My father spoke to her back.

"This is some kind of hoax," he said. "I don't know how that lady is doing this, but I'm not going to let her get away with it. Jesus, Delia! You and I both know I grew up in this house . . . That is the real reality."

"That's what you've told me."

"And now you don't believe me either?"

Mama shut off the tap. "I was joking. Of course, I know you grew up in this house. No sane person would lie about growing up in a dump like this. But I also know what it's like to be dispossessed—to have the landlord show up in the middle of the night and change the locks—and I'm going to be prepared this time." Mama had been evicted as a little girl when her dad's cigar store went broke. "Once bitten, twice shy."

My father hurled his brandy glass into the face of the refrigerator. "You should see a fucking psychiatrist," he shouted. "Just because your father got you thrown out on your ass at eight or ten or whatever doesn't mean you need to take that bitch's side."

Papa rarely used profanity—that was Mama's sphere of expertise—so his outburst warned me that his moorings might be loosening. His frustrations manifested themselves in a different—but equally pernicious—manner the next day, when a Canadian couple with a toddler requested a tour. The wife wore a tie-dyed T-shirt and acid-wash jeans; the husband boasted a bushy beard and the arms of a lumberjack. They couldn't have been much younger than my parents.

"I was wondering," asked Bushy Beard, "but do you have a family rate? Fifty dollars is a bit steep for our budget."

My father leaned over the porch railing. "No tours today," he said. "Sorry."

Bushy Beard called to his wife, who was out on the lawn, supervising the toddler, "He says there's no tours today."

The wife drew up beside her husband, steering the child in front of her by its upraised hands. My father had returned to pacing, utterly indifferent to their presence.

"Is it a holiday?" Bushy Beard asked Papa.

A peculiar expression colored Papa's features.

"Nope, not a holiday," he said. "More of a mistake, really. It turns out Einstein didn't actually live here." My father stepped to the edge of the porch, like an old-time politician delivering a speech. "Einstein didn't live anywhere near the ocean," he continued. "In fact, the man hated water; he suffered from chronic hydrophobia. Sub-acute rabies . . . He was bitten by a mad hedgehog as a child and never got over it. The experts say that's why he had such a large brain: swelling from the rabies."

Bushy Beard reached for his wife's hand. Papa was still spinning this bizarre tale as the young family retreated to their vehicle and peeled onto the avenue, forcing him to shout the last few words of narrative.

"You wanted a tour," he shouted after them. "There's your tour!"

By the end of the week, Mama had no choice but to put her contingency plan into action, and a team of Greek movers—handsome, olive-skinned men with long hair—loaded our furniture into a van. That also necessitated a very unpleasant conversation between her and Dr. Arcaya. I'd concealed myself in the downstairs foyer to spy on them, and I'll never forget how pitiable the elderly veterinarian looked, like one of the Belgian refugees in our fifth-grade history textbook, when he said, "We did not deserve such treatment." I later learned that nearly all of the money from the short-lived touring enterprise went to compensate the tenants.

On the night of July 30, Mama made one last inspection of the house and then divided our remaining belongings between the two cars for the five-hour drive to Aunt Claire's in Laurendale. Very little of value remained in the vacant rooms, but my mother hadn't packed any of the "Einstein" memorabilia. The cluttered chalkboard still stood in the barren kitchen. The jar with the pig fetus rested above the mantelpiece.

In the driveway, my father looked up at the house and cried out at the façade, "I did grow up in this house, goddammit. My cousin Benjamin choked to death in the breakfast room. My mother had her stroke in the upstairs bath. I've lived here for forty-two years, and I had mumps here, and scarlet fever, and two bouts of pneumonia, and no lousy trick can change that." He turned suddenly from the house to Mama. "Don't look at me like that," he shouted. "It can't."

I squeezed Nadine's wrist.

My sister looked up at me and asked, "Is this what nuclear winter is like?"

That marked the end of Papa's clever ideas. He stopped filing patents and never again mentioned animal-to-human translation, self-proofreading printing presses, or typewriters that generated text in two languages simultaneously. After he wrote a letter of apology to his former boss at Bell Labs (upon Mama's insistence), AT&T proved willing to invite him back to their Murray Hill headquarters—where he muddled along on rather prosaic assignments for another fifteen years. To my knowledge, he never mentioned the house at 2467 South Ocean Avenue or Hager's Head or Albert Einstein ever again. When Nadine once asked him about it—for a family history album she was compiling in eleventh grade—he insisted he didn't remember very much about the place and retreated onto the stoop for fresh air. My parents had moved to an apartment in Newark by then, a cramped walk-up in the Ironbound district. The air smelled of rotting shellfish from the Portuguese bistro across the alley—for me, during my increasingly infrequent visits, a taunting reminder of the fresh salt air of my childhood. I'd become an investigative journalist by then—and, ironically, I'd given up on asking my parents all but the most superficial questions.

All of that was still far into the future, of course, that torrid morning we left the Jersey Shore for Aunt Claire's row house in Virginia. My father followed the taillights of Mama's Plymouth, glassy eyed and silent. He didn't say a word until we were twenty minutes outside Baltimore and the Pontiac blew out a tire. Then the vehicle limped over to the shoulder, and he retrieved the spare from the trunk. Mama found the jack stashed in a compartment under the hood and peppered him with instructions.

Papa stopped tightening lug nuts at one point and looked up from his knees.

"You were right," he said to Mama. "You were right, and I was wrong."

"Some good that does," griped my mother. "Now make sure you don't screw those nuts on too tight in case we need to take them off again."

Papa slammed his wrench against the pavement. "I'm admitting I screwed up. I'm not trying to argue, Delia . . . Is it so hard to let me apologize?"

But she didn't yield. "So you were wrong and I was right. That doesn't change anything," Mama said. She stood arms akimbo at the cusp of the interstate, flushed in the sweltering heat, while her sweat-stained husband crouched beside her on the steaming black asphalt. And this was the moment when an eleven-year-old schoolgirl named Natalie Scragg first recognized the painful difference that would forever separate her from her mother: given a choice, Natalie preferred having a house, while her mother preferred having a fight.

"We all know you were wrong, Bryce," said her mother, including her daughters in her condemnation. "That's so not the point."

THE ROD OF ASCLEPIUS

A FIRST PULSE OF MEMORY: my father, broad-shouldered and dashing, sliding his arms into a long white coat that smells of bleach. It is springtime in St. Arnac, a balmy Sunday afternoon snowing crab apple petals. We've parked in the physicians-only lot atop the roof of the hospital's garage, the same hospital where, the previous Thanksgiving, my pregnant mother died of a ruptured uterus. What my six-year-old self doesn't realize then, though it is clear to me now, is that this may be the first time my father has left our apartment in several months, that I am witnessing the man emerge from a winter-long twilight of raw anger. He drapes his stethoscope around his neck and retrieves his leather bag from the trunk of our Oldsmobile. "Are you ready to change the world, princess?" he asks. At that moment, I am suddenly persuaded that the world does indeed require changing, that the entire cosmos yearns for radical transformation. Vigorous nods earn me a kiss on the forehead.

My father leads me by hand across the broad granite plaza, colonized with lunching nurses and orderlies on smoke breaks, where statues of North Carolina's war heroes guard the revolving doors. At the security desk, a red-faced officer with a greasy comb-over greets my father with a genial, "Hi, doc," and then salutes me with a more formal, "Good afternoon, ma'am." I am still too young to distinguish personal from business relationships, friends from sociable strangers—it will be another year or so before I realize, in an innocence-shattering blast, that our postman is paid to deliver the mail—so I swell with pride as the officer waves us past the visitors waiting to register, believing a personal honor is being bestowed on my father, not realizing the privilege is afforded all white-coated medical gentry.

We ride the elevator to the top. The doors open directly onto the lobby of the VIP atrium, where angelfish and gouramis cross paths in a colossal aquarium, while a sad-eyed pianist plays cocktail lounge standards on a baby grand. Panoramic windows reveal the rolling, sun-drenched hills of the Piedmont and the wood-shingled rooftops of St. Arnac's commercial district—an assortment of family-owned specialty shops, like my Aunt Hannah's millinery, which have since been swallowed by suburban Greensboro. Papa's grip is tight on my hand. He crosses the lounge and strides briskly down the adjacent corridor, practically sweeping me along the tiles behind him. We pass the nursing station where, beneath the cardiac monitors, a solitary aide reads a magazine. A whiff of disinfectant hangs in the stagnant air.

And then—without warning—Papa veers through an open door. Suddenly, we stand inside a patient's private room, the temporary home of an ancient, one-legged man dwarfed by his own wheelchair. The man's truncated knee is wrapped in gauze, suggesting a recent amputation. At his side, perched at the foot of the tidy bed, sits an equally wizened woman. To my surprise, my father apologizes for disturbing the couple, and we retreat back into the corridor.

A moment later, we've entered another room. Here, a skeletal woman watches television from a stack of pillows. She cannot be much older than my father, but her eyes are sunken, and her pale skin drapes off the bones of her face. On the end table, two photographs depict the same woman in the full bloom of health. In one picture, a handsome man clasps his arm around her waist; in the other, she cradles an infant. A basket of fruit and gourmet items—still wrapped—sits on the radiator. When the woman sees my father, she uses the remote control to lower the TV's volume.

"Have you seen Dr. Hagerman?" she asks.

Papa touches the woman's shoulder to offer reassurance. "I'm covering for Dr. Hagerman today," he informs her in the same confident voice he uses to comfort me when I have a nightmare.

"He swore he'd be here before noon," says the woman.

"I'm sorry. Dr. Hagerman had an emergency. Something personal."

The emaciated woman seems partially assuaged. Papa opens his leather bag and fills a syringe. "We need to give you some blood thinner," he explains. "Dr. Hagerman was concerned about your most recent laboratory values, especially the risk for spontaneous clotting." As he speaks, my father rolls up the sleeve of the woman's gown; she winces, and the injection is over. "That should do the trick," he says. "Dr. Hagerman will be here to see you in the morning."

My father discards the syringe and removes his gloves. Even as he shuts the clasps on his bag, the woman drifts into slumber, a tranquil smile settled on her lips. We are already halfway down the corridor when an alarm bell sounds from the woman's room; as we approach the nursing station, a junior physician in aqua scrubs charges past us headed in the opposite direction.

We traverse the VIP atrium again and descend the elevator to the lobby. My father and the red-faced officer exchange another greeting. I feel anxious, but I cannot say why. Out on the granite plaza, a swarm of starlings blankets the austere statues of Confederate generals and colonels.

My father lifts me into his powerful arms.

"We went to the top floor," he explains, "because that's where the doctors' wives and mothers go when they get sick." Papa's eyes are level with mine, his nose so close I could touch it. "Don't be afraid to ask your father questions, Lauren," he adds. "I want this to be a learning experience."

⚛

Or maybe that is not a first pulse of memory. Quite possibly, that visit to the hospital occurs after Aunt Henrietta comes to live with us. I can vividly remember her boyfriend—one of my aunt's many boyfriends—transporting her suitcases from the trunk of his car into the guest bedroom. She'll be twenty-eight that summer, five years younger than my father, and stunningly gorgeous. I don't recall if Papa is also present that afternoon, but I do remember the two of them arguing bitterly a few days later while Aunt Henrietta drains bottles of whiskey into the sink. Only years in the future did I discover that my aunt's arrival hadn't been Papa's choice: it was part of the custody arrangement he had agreed to with Guilford County's Bureau of Child Welfare after I went truant from kindergarten.

If my aunt resented her premature summons to child-rearing, I never recall her showing it, although she remained committed to putting me "to good use." After school lets out for the summer, I accompany her to the millinery each morning, where she assigns me various "constructive" tasks around the bustling shop. Some days, I sort ribbons or buckles. On other occasions, I unwrap exotic hats that arrive from the warehouse packed in newsprint. Yet I spend most of my time with the young African-American fitters who "mind the store" while my aunt enjoys half-day lunch breaks with her various suitors. One of these shop girls, an olive-skinned teenager named

Lila, takes a particular fancy to me because, as she phrases it, "We're both orphans, so we have to look out for each other."

"I'm not an orphan," I insist. "My father is still alive."

Lila hugs me to her ample bosom. "Silly girl," she says. "Fathers don't count."

What I do know with certainty is that our visit to the hospital precedes my conversation with Aunt Henrietta about what I hope to become when I grow up. That talk occurs while we're on an excursion to pick peaches. My aunt is dating a dental student whose family owns vast orchards south of Asheboro, so I'm ensconced between the two of them on the front seat of the young man's Cadillac. The open windows bring a gentle breeze and with it the scent of drying alfalfa. My aunt's boyfriend, whose marriage proposal she will soon reject, has urged her to invite me along on this outing; he is doing his utmost to keep me entertained—to prove, I suppose, that he'd make a good father.

He addresses me in a high-pitched, sing-song voice, as though I am an infant and not a rising first grader. "So, young lady, do you have any career plans yet?"

"I don't know," I answer.

Aunt Henrietta asks, "Do you know what a 'career' is?"

"Nope."

Her boyfriend tries again. "What do you want to be when you grow up?"

I fold my arms across my chest.

"Would you like to be a princess?" he asks. "Or how about a mermaid?"

Both sound like perfectly reasonable occupations to my six-year-old mind, but the young man's tone makes me feel contrary. "I want to be a doctor," I announce.

"Nothing wrong with that," says the dental student. He is grinning. "We could use more lady doctors."

Aunt Henrietta also appears amused. "That's the first I've heard of this," she says. "I'm curious, Lauren. Why do you want to be a doctor?"

I don't have a good answer. Even when I apply to medical school two decades later, my various justifications—to help people, to expand human knowledge, even to save lives—somehow never seem adequate. I suppose the real reason I become a physician is because I can't imagine doing anything else, but it takes another thirty years of reflection to reach even that degree of insight. The explanation I give my aunt is far more concrete: "Because Papa is a doctor."

The dental student flashes my aunt a puzzled look. I sense that I've said something wrong, but I'm honestly not sure what.

"Your papa isn't a doctor," says Aunt Henrietta, her voice kind but firm. "What on earth would ever give you that idea?"

I sense that I must not mention our visit to the hospital, that my father will want that to remain our secret. "I don't know," I say.

"Her father was an architect," my aunt informs her date. "Before."

The young man nods sympathetically. "Does she know about . . . ?"

He lets his sentence trail away, as though the word mother were toxic.

"She knows," says Aunt Henrietta. "But I don't think she really understands."

֍

I can't be certain whether my father visits the hospital again on his own, but the next time we visit together, it is already late summer, and the corn along the county highway towers over his Oldsmobile. Instead of the community hospital in St. Arnac, we drive forty-five minutes to the freshly minted women's clinic in Greensboro. My aunt is away for the weekend with her new boyfriend, a veterinarian, who will soon become my Uncle Conrad, and will later become my former Uncle Conrad, and will eventually move to Florida and open a theme park featuring exotic animals. Papa has finally mustered the wherewithal to warn me against discussing our hospital field trips with his sister, but when I tell him that I already know they are our secret, he grins. "Your mother would be so proud of you, princess," he says. Later, as we pull into a metered space opposite the clinic, he adds, "Never forget why we're here, Lauren. This is for your mother." And his voice is compelling, although even at the age of six, I'm already aware that his thinking itself is muddled, that my mother never set foot inside the women's clinic in Greensboro.

The security guard on duty, a dour young woman, takes her job far more seriously than the jolly old-timers in St. Arnac. She asks my father for his ID card, and, when he apologizes that he has left it in his car, she suggests with a firm civility that he retrieve it. "If you insist," he replies genially. But rather than return to the Oldsmobile, we circle the building until we arrive at the ambulance bay. "Pretend you're sleeping, princess," instructs Papa, scooping me up and carrying me into the emergency room as though I were an accident victim. A genuine trauma patient has arrived ahead of us, so the ER is a maelstrom of clattering equipment and frantic resuscitation efforts. An elderly woman pleads with God for her son's recovery at top volume while medics shear the clothing off a blood-drenched body. Nobody takes much notice of Papa as he strolls confidently through a graveyard of gurneys into the belly of the hospital. Soon enough, we've found ourselves another private room on an upper floor of the building.

This room appears far fancier than the one we visited in St. Arnac; oak-paneled walls and rosewood furniture lend it the ambience of a private library. Years later, when I reconstruct these events from newspaper articles, I learn that the room belongs not to a physician's relative but to a physician herself: Dr. Jane Barnwell, the forty-two-year-old head of pediatric nephrology, who has suffered minor complications following the birth of her first child and is being held overnight for observation. Fortunately for us, Dr. Barnwell sleeps soundly. Papa takes great care not to wake her. He loads his syringe in her private bathroom, instructs me to wait for him and not to make any noise, and then returns several seconds later and tucks the spent needle and rubber gloves into his leather bag.

"All done, princess," he says. "Good job."

He snaps shut the satchel and gives the room a final once-over. Dr. Barnwell doesn't look any different than she did ten minutes earlier, except her chest no longer heaves.

"What do you say we stop for ice cream on the way home?" asks Papa.

"Strawberry?"

"Whatever your heart desires," agrees my father.

We exit the hospital as we entered, through the emergency room, again drawing no notice. On the avenue, however, a squad car with flashing lights has drawn up behind the Oldsmobile. One of the officers remains seated in the vehicle, while the other stands on the sidewalk, comforting a distraught young woman in a burgundy smock. The woman has fiery red hair like my own mother's and wide, child-bearing hips; if she wore less makeup, she'd be prettier.

I am still at an age when I find the presence of police officers to be reassuring rather than threatening, yet that afternoon I suspect their arrival bodes trouble. Papa, however, does not appear at all unnerved by their presence.

"Is something wrong, officer?" he asks.

The officer looks up. "Your car?"

"I'm afraid so," says Papa. "Did I park in the wrong place?"

"Yes, you did," says the cop. He's a gaunt bulrush

of a man who looks as though a strong wind might topple him. "You parked right behind this woman's vehicle."

I now notice that glass shards blanket the asphalt, remnants of the Oldsmobile's left headlight. A deep cleft forks the vehicle's front bumper, which buckles over the grill. The redheaded woman has apparently backed her car into ours.

"I'm so sorry, doctor," the woman apologizes to Papa, who still sports his white coat. "I honestly don't know what happened. I thought I was in drive, and I must have been in reverse, and I can't believe I could ever be so stupid . . ." She sounds as though she is seconds away from tears.

"Not a big deal," says Papa. He turns to the slender cop. "Officer, is there any way we can forget this ever happened?"

These days I practice medicine in Manhattan, and asking a question like that in this city can get a person arrested, but three decades ago, in Greensboro, the rules are more flexible. The slender officer steps over to the patrol car to confer with his partner. The second cop, an older man with a shock of white hair, climbs out of the vehicle.

"What are you going to do about the insurance?" he asks.

"Absolutely nothing," replies Papa. "It's not worth it. I'll just patch her up in my garage and she'll be as good as new. If I can operate on a human brain, I can operate on a busted bumper. Anyway, there's no reason this lady's insurance rates should skyrocket over a minor accident."

The veteran cop shrugs. "Suit yourself, doc," he says.

The older cop nods to the younger cop, and the pair depart into the urban web of Greensboro, leaving us alone with the grateful redhead. "I don't know how to thank you," she says. "I've never even been in an accident before. I'd offer to buy you lunch in the cafeteria sometime, but this is the last day of my rotation. I'm a nursing student—did I mention that?—and I go back to the hospital in Winston-Salem next week." She looks at Papa, who hasn't said a word, and blushes. "Oh, goodness. I'm talking too much, aren't I?"

"Not at all. Why don't we buy you lunch? Right now."

The nursing student, whose name I later learn is Suzanne, glances at me with apprehension. "Won't this girl's mother worry if you're not home on time?"

"This girl's mother," replies Papa, "is dead."

Suzanne's expression flutters from shock to sympathy, but I can see a bit of relief in her face, as well. "I'm sorry," she says.

"Not half as sorry as I am," says Papa. "But now that we've broken the ice, how do you two beautiful ladies feel about barbecued chicken?"

Papa's mood improves considerably after he starts dating Suzanne Shale. We drive out to Winston-Salem every Friday and spend the weekend at her cozy, cluttered apartment two blocks from Wake Forest's medical center. At the time, I take for granted that Papa brings me along with him on these romantic getaways; in hindsight, I've come to recognize that Suzanne's physical similarity to my late mother is not a coincidence—that my father, in some perverse way, hopes to reconstruct the family he has lost. For her part, Suzanne is twenty-four years old and thrilled to be dating a neurosurgeon—even one endowed with so much integrity that he refuses to help her with her pharmacology homework. That doesn't stop her from begging for assistance, especially as she is barely passing her exams.

One evening, at a crowded steak house near the undergraduate campus, Papa nearly makes a fatal mistake while resisting her pleas. It is my seventh birthday dinner—my second seventh birthday dinner, because my father never brings Suzanne to St. Arnac—and he is working his way down the cocktail menu.

"What are you going to do when you're alone with a sick patient?" Papa asks her. "Are you going to phone me from the hospital so I can convert cc's into milliliters for you?"

Suzanne appears confused. "Cc's are milliliters," she says.

Papa smiles. "Just checking," he replies. "So they are teaching you something in that nursing program, after all."

I am impressed—even at age seven—by my father's talent for deception, his ability to meet every challenge and contingency. However, I am still too young to give much thought to long-term consequences. In hindsight, I find myself wondering whether he has given any mind to his endgame, to what will happen when Suzanne insists on meeting his family or planning a wedding. Does he really think he can keep his ruse going forever? Does he care? Twenty-five years later, hoping to glean some insight, I write to Suzanne Shale—now Suzanne Stanley—but my father's ex-girlfriend responds with a curt note asking me to leave her alone. I can't say I blame her.

Yet that autumn, for a brief interval, the three of us do feel like a family. We purchase a trio of pumpkins for Halloween, and while Papa and I carve jack-o'-lanterns, Suzanne bakes pies from the pulp. We go hiking in the foothills north of the city to view the foliage at its most colorful. In early November, we enjoy a weekend road trip to Virginia, where Suzanne introduces us to her mother. Thanks to Papa's seven-digit malpractice settlement with the insurance company, he has no need to return to his architecture firm. In his leisure, he drives me to school every morning.

Our hospital visits drift into memory, so I am caught entirely off guard one weekend near Thanksgiving, when Papa rouses me from my slumber in Suzanne's apartment for a "medical emergency."

"They need a consult on a bullet wound. A very tricky case," my father tells Suzanne. "We'll be back as soon as we can."

At first, I assume we are returning to St. Arnac. Instead, we drive five blocks to Baptist Hospital and park in the staff-only lot. My father adjusts his necktie with the help of the rearview mirror and then slides his arms into his white coat. He pins a Wake Forest ID card to his lapel—a forgery, I imagine, but it looks real enough.

"Can I ask a question?" I ask.

"What, princess?"

My stomach flutters. "How long are we going to keep visiting hospitals for?"

"Until we're done," he says.

All these years later, I'm still not sure what he means.

By now, of course, I know what to expect. So I am not at all surprised when we climb the stairs to the VIP floor and work our medical magic, as Papa calls it, on a middle-aged woman with a nasty rash across her forearms and neck. Yet rather than making a quick getaway, my father ducks into a second room and injects an elderly man who is listening to a baseball game on his transistor radio. We "treat" two more patients before a "Code 1000" is called over the PA system. Thirty minutes later, we're eating French fries at a café and rehearsing our alibi for Suzanne.

"We've changed the world quite a lot for one day, Lauren," says Papa. "I couldn't have done it without you."

I fill my mouth with French fries and ketchup.

Papa asks, "Let's review, princess. Why are we doing this?"

"For Mama."

That is precisely what Papa wants to hear—what I have been coached to say— and he beams with approval. To strangers, he appears to be just another doting father accompanying his daughter out for a snack.

"Tell me one more thing, princess," he says. "What have you learned today?"

In the absence of guidance, I answer honestly. "I want to be a doctor."

The words are hardly out of my mouth when the sting of my father's palm sets my cheek aflame. I am too shocked to cry. The cashier at the café register flashes Papa a look of intense hostility; an elderly lady at a nearby table glances away. Nobody intervenes, of course: this is long before child abuse becomes a public concern. That does not make my face hurt any less.

"Doctors are the enemy. Never forget that," says Papa. "Is that clear?"

"Okay," I say. "I'm sorry."

"I didn't mean to hurt you, princess," he says, his tone gentle once more. "But I'm counting on you. Mama is counting on you. You won't disappoint us, will you?"

I promise that I won't let him down, and he never raises a hand against me again. Of course, I never give him reason to do so. By the time we return to Suzanne's apartment that evening, my upper lip is swollen—an injury we blame on a doorknob.

"She's still the most beautiful girl in the world," says Papa. "But in the future, she has to be more careful."

☙

I am very careful from that day forward: so painstakingly careful that I take to eavesdropping on my father, amassing a secret stash of knowledge to avoid any more mistakes. After bedtime at Suzanne's apartment, I tiptoe into the foyer and press my tiny ear against the ventilation duct. From beyond the groaning of pipes comes the murmur of pillow talk. It's like having a radio broadcast directly from inside my father's head. That is how I learn that they are arguing, that Papa refuses to have the nursing student to St. Arnac for Christmas. "I can't handle it yet," he insists. "It reminds me of Ellen. I'm sorry." Never before, as far back as I can remember, has Papa called my mother by her given name; it takes me a moment to realize whom he's talking about.

"Is that the only reason?" asks Suzanne.

"What's that supposed to mean?" demands my father. "Not wanting to be reminded of my slaughtered wife isn't a good enough reason?"

Suzanne responds in a soothing tone; I cannot make out her words. But her volume rises as she says, "All I want is the truth. I love you. You can trust me."

A long pause follows. I can hear footsteps, presumably Papa's, pacing the hardwood floor. "What are you driving at?" he finally asks.

"I want to be a part of whatever you're a part of, Phil," begs Suzanne. "I'm going to put my cards on the table: I know you're not a brain surgeon. None of the girls who've rotated through Greensboro Women's this fall has ever heard of you . . . But I'm fine with whatever you are: an undercover journalist, or an FBI agent, even a Russian spy.

After six months together, I have a right to know."

This is Papa's opportunity to save himself. Obviously, he doesn't need to reveal that he murders physicians' relatives as a hobby, a revelation that blows past the limits of Suzanne's commitment. He merely must admit that he's a widowed architect with no medical training; I don't know how he'll explain away the white coat, but I'm confident that doing so is well within my father's capabilities. What will happen, I wonder, if he puts his hospital career behind us? Alas, I never find out.

Mattress springs creak at a distance, announcing that Papa has settled onto the bed beside Suzanne. He may have his hand on her knee or her bare thigh.

"You do have a right to know," says Papa. "But I can't tell you."

"Phil—"

"Hear me out," he continues. "You're right. I'm not a brain surgeon—or at least I'm not a brain surgeon at Greensboro Women's. I wish I could tell you what I am doing at the hospital, but I can't. It's not that I don't trust you. Or love you. But telling you would put you in danger, and it would put my project in danger, and people's lives are at stake." I doubt so many falsehoods have been concealed with so much truth. "You'll have to trust me, Suzanne. Can you do that?"

"I don't know. That's a lot to swallow," she replies. "And Christmas?"

"Not this year," says Papa. "I have my reasons."

Suzanne responds with a gust of sobbing, then

a high-pitched wail that breaks periodically against my father's protestations of devotion; I tiptoe back to my own bedroom and cry myself to sleep.

In the morning, a Sunday, Suzanne cooks up a pancake feast on the griddle. She seems less chatty than usual; otherwise, she appears as cheerful and affectionate as ever. When she walks us to the car after breakfast, she kisses Papa on the lips and reminds him to call her when we arrive home safely. Then she hugs me. It is a raw, overcast day in mid-December—the sort of day when hugs always feel the most loving—and a light dusting of snow still blankets yards and hedges. I remember the warmth of that hug because that is the last time I ever see Suzanne Shale.

A final vestige of memory: my father, slumped and intoxicated, fumbling to unsnap the clasps on his satchel. Sixteen days have elapsed since our return from Winston-Salem, sixteen days since Suzanne Shale has delivered her ultimatum. If she does not come to St. Arnac for Christmas, she'll leave my father. But we share a holiday supper with only Aunt Henrietta and my future uncle, who depart early the next morning for a week-long vacation on the Gulf Coast. It is now December 27, approaching evening, but Papa has made no effort to turn on the lights.

We sit at the kitchen table. Papa has grilled me a cheese sandwich and poured me a tall glass of chocolate milk. I chew in silence, watching him unpack his medical supplies, bracing myself for another visit to the hospital, but Papa isn't planning any more excursions.

"I think it's time to teach you something, princess," he says. "You still want to be a doctor, right? Do you want to learn how to give an injection?"

"I don't know."

Papa manages to unsnap the clasps on his bag. "What I'm going to do, princess," he says, "is fill this syringe with sodium chloride. Salt water. Totally harmless, but excellent practice. All I need you to do is give your father an injection."

"I don't want to," I say.

Papa's expression hardens.

"I'm not asking you, Lauren. I'm telling you."

My father insists that I pull my chair up alongside him. He is far too drunk to fill the syringe, too drunk even to hold the needle steady, so I am forced to draw the fluid out of the bottle on my own. My fingers ache from the multiple attempts. Nausea builds under my tongue. Papa clenches his free hand around my other wrist; even if I wish to flee, I cannot.

"All right, princess," he says. "Just like a doctor."

His breath, his body, the entire kitchen stinks of whiskey.

I insert the bevel and draw back the plunger. I know that the syringe contains more than sodium chloride—that even as the toxic contents fill my father's veins, he is sharing with me his final gift: the horror and thrill of saving lives.

SHARING THE HOSTAGE

WE'RE ON OUR FIFTH DATE—if you can still call them dates after you've been sleeping together for two weeks—and I've driven Maddie out to Flamingo Beach for a heart-to-heart. Flamingo Beach isn't actually a beach at all, but a rocky patch of public shoreline on the northern coast of Long Island Sound. Hermit crabs scamper between tidal pools. Across the water, New York's skyscrapers shimmer like bejeweled sea creatures under the bright August sun. Obviously, there are no flamingos—only an outcropping of pink granite that once reminded some Yankee mariner of tropical birds. As teenagers, my friends gathered here on summer nights to smoke marijuana and plan world conquest. On September 12, 2001, I retreated to these rocks for my first glimpse of the transformed Manhattan skyline.

So a decade later, at forty-two, it seems like a safe place to share the secret that has, for all practical purposes, ended my last two relationships. And this time, because Maddie cannot drive, I'll at least have the car ride back to the city to convince her to see me again.

"So what's the catch?" asks Maddie. At thirty-six, she's also a relationship skeptic. "Everything is going so well, I feel as though there must be a catch."

We've spread out a blanket in the shade of a long-abandoned boathouse, and Maddie's head is resting on my lap.

"You honestly want to know? My sister steals babies."

Maddie's grin melts quickly as she senses that I'm not joking. She sits up, her long auburn hair dappled with twigs. "For real?"

"Not anymore. Now she gets a shot of Haldol in the ass every month and attends a day program for schizophrenics," I explain. "But before that, Eileen was arrested three times for baby-snatching. Given a choice between following the law or the voices in her head, the voices win out every time."

Maddie squeezes my forearm. She's a massage therapist, and she has a gift for expressing herself with her touch. "That's crummy, but it's not exactly a catch," she says. "What I mean is, your sister's illness isn't going to ruin our relationship."

"She's not the only one. I have an aunt like that. And three cousins. We've got something wrong with our genes," I continue. "They don't steal babies, of course. But they've all spent time in the state hospital. Lots of time.

One of them jumped out of a moving ambulance and nearly died." I draw a deep breath and focus my eyes on a far-off water-skier, unwilling to meet Maddie's gaze. The water-skier sports an orange life vest. He's holding the line with only one hand, rising and dipping with the current. "So there's the catch. I'm not willing to risk having children—not biologically." I'm still trailing the water-skier across the open channel; suddenly he loses his grip and wipes out. "This is going to be a deal breaker, isn't it?"

"A moving ambulance," echoes Maddie. "That's high stakes."

"High?" I ask. "Or too high?"

"We can work through it later," she replies. "We'll figure something out."

I'm thrilled there is going to be a later. For most childless women over thirty-five, including my last two girlfriends, later is now. I'm seized with an urge to embrace Maddie, but she has her arms wrapped around her bare knees, and she's staring pensively into the waves.

"I've got a secret of my own. Worse than yours," she says. "Promise you're not going to get mad—or laugh at me."

I am practically shaking with relief: I've played my "no children" card, and Maddie hasn't run off—so, short of a permanent vow of celibacy, there is little she can possibly say at the moment to upset me. "What could be worse than a second cousin who thinks the United Nations spies on her through her pacemaker?"

My companion remains silent. Overhead, a cloud briefly obliterates the sun. When Maddie finally speaks, her voice, always soft, is nearly lost in the breaking surf. "I meet my ex-husband every Saturday afternoon as part of our joint-custody arrangement," she says. "That's why I couldn't get together last weekend."

"You have a kid?"

"Not exactly," says Maddie. "Fred is a tortoise."

She turns to face me—to gauge my reaction—and I dig my teeth into my lip.

"Don't you dare laugh at me," she warns.

"Who's laughing?" I ask.

"I've had Fred for almost six years," says Maddie. "We adopted him on our honeymoon. At a pet shop in New Orleans. And now Michael has taken him hostage. The prick doesn't give a damn about Fred—but he knows that I do—and he's holding onto him for revenge."

I am aware Maddie has been in the process of finalizing a divorce, but until now I have not asked for any details. "Can't you take him to court?"

"I did take him to court—and I lost," snaps Maddie. "Michael should have won an Academy Award for all the bullshit he spewed about his love of animals. On top of that, he had some client of his with a PhD in reptile biology write a letter on Fordham University stationery saying that relocating a tortoise can be disruptive to its health." Maddie has balled her delicate hands into fists. "And do you know what the judge said? He said, 'I'm all for equality, but you can't exactly divide a turtle in half.'"

You can if you want to make soup, I think. I do not say this.

"That's awful," I say. "But why would I be mad at you?"

"I'm getting to that part. Michael still wants to get back together with me, and I honestly don't feel comfortable going to our house—his house—alone anymore." Maddie intertwines her fingers with mine, as though in a collective prayer. "Can you please come with me next Saturday?"

"Let me get this straight: you want me to spend my Saturday chaperoning you and your ex-husband while you have a playdate with a turtle?"

"Not just next Saturday. Every Saturday," counters Maddie. "I promise it won't be that bad. You can even wait in the car."

Three days later, we're driving up the parkway toward Yonkers. That's where Maddie's ex-husband lives—technically her almost ex-husband, as there are still papers to be notarized—and where Maddie lived until four months ago. My judicial externship is finished for the summer, and I won't start law school classes again until after Labor Day, so I am largely a man without responsibilities. Before law school, I spent nearly two decades pursuing my childhood dream, eking out a living as a professional ventriloquist— and failing abysmally—so I am also a man who appreciates his own limitations. My wooden dummy, Dr. Whipple, sits limp on a closet shelf behind last spring's study guides to contracts and torts. Maddie knows nothing of his existence.

That's the challenge of dating this late in the game: a whole lot of backstory. For all I know, Fred the Tortoise is the tip of the iceberg. Maybe Maddie visits other hostile exes to check up on Lester the Llama and Orville the Ostrich.

"Thank you for doing this," says Maddie. "You can't imagine how much better this is than taking the public bus."

"You'll have your chance to make it up to me," I answer. "Next time Eileen runs off with someone's twins, guess who's visiting the psych ward at Bellevue?"

"Sure thing," she agrees. "I'll even knit her a straightjacket."

I'm grateful that Maddie can find humor in my sister's illness. Several of my past loves avoided mentioning her at all—as though the less they spoke about Eileen, the more likely she was to evaporate. Yet that was infinitely preferable to the reaction of the aspiring anthropologist I dated at NYU who insisted that schizophrenia was a gift from the gods, and who kept trying to convince me that Eileen's erratic conduct was "a sane response to an insane world." I adore my sister, but even she can find the humor in her own antics—at least when she's on meds. When I told her that I was escorting Maddie to visit Fred, she joked, Why don't you just steal him?

Maddie directs me through the back streets of Yonkers, down blocks of low-slung brick duplexes. Families barbecue on cluttered front lawns. Bathtub madonnas and immaculately tended geraniums warn interlopers like us that this neighborhood takes seriously its commitments to faith and honest labor. Maddie's ex manages a roofing company. She has told me repeatedly that my best quality is that I'm "nothing like Michael," but only now—surrounded by garden gnomes and year-round Christmas lights—do I fully realize how different the roofer's world is from my own.

Michael's house is modest and nondescript. The bumper sticker on the Plymouth in the driveway reads "IF WE QUIT VOTING, WILL THEY ALL GO AWAY?" When I park across from his mailbox, the children in the opposite yard eye us warily, as though they fear we might steal their tricycles.

Maddie kisses me. "Wait here. I'll call if I need your help," she says. "And try to look intimidating, just in case Michael peeks out the window." Seconds later, the seat beside me is empty. Maddie opens the front door of Michael's house with her own key, and I am alone.

I do make a brief attempt to look intimidating, but I give up quickly. My only two life skills are throwing my voice and crafting legal briefs—neither of which is likely to prove particularly useful against a man who was dishonorably discharged from the Coast Guard for bare-knuckle boxing. Fortunately, the shades in Michael's bay windows are drawn. Deep down, I suspect Maddie's fears are overblown: her ex-husband may be a jerk who holds reptiles captive for leverage, but there's no evidence that he'd actually hurt her. I open McCormick on Evidence, hoping to get a head start on my fall reading. When I look up—in response to a slamming door—Maddie's ex is walking straight toward me.

Michael is shorter than I'd expected, but broad shouldered. He wears his gunmetal hair in a ponytail. Reflective sunglasses mask his eyes. The notion hits me that my predecessor may be carrying a handgun, but by the time I gain the wherewithal to consider fleeing, the enraged roofer is already rapping his fingers against the driver's-side window. I lower it one-third of the way.

"You her new boyfriend?" he demands.

"I'm with Maddie," I say, "if that's what you mean."

Michael rests his fingertips along the top edge of the window—as though daring me to close it on his hand. "Here's the deal. I've got a job to do today, but don't you even think of setting foot inside my house. Maddie has my permission. You don't. So that makes it fucking trespassing. I'll know. And I will call the cops. Got that?"

A braver man might raise the issue of the captive turtle at this juncture, but I fear that if I utter something clever like "Let my tortoise go," the roofer will break off the mirrors of my Buick. "Nobody's trespassing on your property," I say.

"Good," he shoots back. "Don't test me."

Michael sizes me up one last time, and my thumb is already on the electric window switch when his entire face ignites with shock. "Holy shit!" he exclaims—and now I'm certain that he's going to shoot me. I close my eyes, steeling my body for the fatal bullet. "Jesus Christ," he mutters. "Jesus fucking Christ."

I open my eyes. Michael appears shaken.

"I know you," he says. "You're the guy with the talking

doll."

It takes me a moment to realize he means Dr. Whipple.

"It's definitely you. I don't forget faces," he continues. "We brought my niece to see you on her seventh birthday. What was the name of that damn thing? Something for Idiots?"

"Ventriloquism for Dummies," I offer. "It's a play on words."

"This is fucking unbelievable," Michael mutters. "Maddie leaves me for a guy who does puppet shows."

It's only a matter of time, I realize, before this guy informs Maddie that I used to help a mahogany surgeon perform invisible brain surgery on second graders. I say, "I hope your niece enjoyed my show."

"Don't be a wise ass," replies Michael. "Anyway, I'm leaving. You do not have my permission to go inside. Don't forget that."

Maddie charges out of the house five minutes later. My girlfriend—I think it's safe to call her that now—has eyeliner streaming down her cheeks, and she's carrying what looks like a damask curtain. She's already buckled into the passenger seat when I first notice the silky reptilian head poking forth from beneath the cloth. Fred the Tortoise's tiny green features display a look of dopey bewilderment. I know this expression well: it's the same face my relatives wear during their first days on the psychiatric ward.

"Drive!" orders Maddie.

"Where to?"

"It doesn't matter. Anywhere."

So I hit the accelerator. I'm acutely aware that I am now an accessory to turtle-napping, that this is the sort of offense that will be hell to explain to the bar examiners. I can easily picture one of those retired judges on the Character and Fitness Committee asking me, So, Mr. Wallace, what precisely was going through your head as you drove off with another man's reptile? How can the citizens of this great state trust you to practice law when we can't even trust you alone with our domestic animals? I will have no good answers. Until the moment that the woman you're sleeping with arrives at your car clutching a pilfered tortoise, you can't predict how you'll react.

"What happened?" I ask.

"I don't know."

"You don't know?"

"I was scrubbing Fred's shell with his prescription cleanser—Michael never bathes him—and I was telling Fred about our relationship, and about how I'd asked you to wait outside for me, and suddenly the unreasonableness of it all overwhelmed me. Through this entire process, I've played by the rules—and the rules always end up favoring Michael. I'm the one who had to find a new place to live. I'm the one who had to find a new job because I had no way of commuting to my old one. The judge didn't even award me half the value of our car. Do you know what the jerk said? He said, 'Your husband has paid off your share of the vehicle by chauffeuring you around for the past six years.' So I heard Michael driving away just now, and something inside me snapped. I'm not going to share Fred anymore. I'm not. I don't care if I have to run off to Mexico."

Maddie clutches the swaddled tortoise to her chest, cradling him like an infant and periodically kissing the scaly rump of his head. It crosses my mind that she has planned this venture long in advance—even that our entire relationship is merely part of a complex scheme whose ultimate goal is reclaiming Fred. But if Maddie thinks I will be ferrying her to Tijuana, or even to New Jersey, she has vastly underestimated my aversion to risk. Bonnie and Clyde, we are not. So I steer us toward the only hideaway I know, Flamingo Beach, hoping that my companion will soon return to her senses. I keep the Buick painstakingly below the speed limit, frustrating the drivers behind me, but I'm not taking any chances with my cold-blooded cargo.

The seashore preserve's parking lot stands nearly empty. I weave around a makeshift plywood barrier and maneuver us along the dusty, meadow-lined trail that leads down to the coastline. Driving here is illegal, as it may disturb breeding whip-poor-wills, but when you're transporting stolen goods, protecting wildfowl becomes a secondary concern.

We pull onto a slab of granite, the shoreline only yards ahead. The tide is full; waves crash violently against stone. I suppose we look like something straight out of an automotive commercial. The only other visible human beings are an elderly couple seated on a wrought iron bench fifty yards up the coast. The woman glowers at us and shakes her head, then returns to her conversation.

"Now what?" I ask.

"It's lunchtime," says Maddie. A few seconds pass until I register that she's talking about Fred's meal, not ours. "I didn't have a chance to feed him before we left, so he must be starving." She removes my favorite mug from the cup holder and pours the last dregs of coffee out the open car door into the tidal mud. "You don't mind if I borrow this. I'm going to hike up to that pasture and dig for earthworms."

"I've had that mug since college," I object.

"Chill out. I'll get you a new one."

A stronger man would yank the mug from her hands. Instead I find myself hoping the tortoise will choke on a worm.

Maddie climbs from the Buick and sets the cloth-encased creature down on the passenger seat. Nothing of the armor-plated creature is visible outside his damask shroud—not so much as one crusty leg. The contraband might easily pass as a well-wrapped box of cigars, or a hunk of farmer cheese, or a stack of paperback books. In short, something entirely innocuous. A year of criminal procedure has assured me that the police cannot inspect my bundle without probable cause. As I take solace in this technicality, the cloth begins to shuffle along the vinyl.

"You can take care of him for a few minutes, can't you?" asks Maddie. "Just keep the air conditioner off and hug him if he seems anxious."

"What about food for us?" I ask.

"I'm too stressed to eat," says Maddie. "When Fred is finished with the earthworms, you can have the leftovers."

"Thanks," I answer. "Let me guess. They're rich in protein."

Maddie reaches into her handbag and fishes out a granola bar. She's now smiling, her makeup-stained face radiating beauty and vulnerability.

"Here," she says. "But save half for dinner."

My girlfriend scrambles over the rocks and disappears into a stand of hickories. I look up the beach: the elderly couple has departed.

Fred and I now have the universe to ourselves.

៘

I remove the blanket from Fred's back; he responds by retracting his head.

"Are you anxious?" I ask. "Would you like a hug?"

The tortoise pokes his head out tentatively. "Do you know what I'd like, buddy?" he answers. "I'd like my liberty."

Fred speaks with an aristocratic, high-pitched British accent—he sounds rather like Winston Churchill orating through helium—and I'm relieved that my talents are still intact. I watch myself in the rearview mirror during Fred's reply, and only a trained professional could detect the muscles moving inside my throat. The idea strikes me that, if I ever return to the stage, a box tortoise might prove an excellent foil for Dr. Whipple. I can already envision the wooden surgeon trying to slice open the reptile's carapace with a plastic scalpel.

"How'd you like to be a star, Freddy, my boy?" I ask. "A household name, Federico. You could be to turtles what Jiminy is to crickets."

"I don't want no fame, mister," pleads Fred, now sounding like a Brooklyn cabbie. "I want my freedom."

"Freedom?" I echo for the benefit of an imaginary audience. "Do you hear that, folks? He says he wants his freedom."

The more I think about freeing Fred, however, the less crazy the idea seems. At some point, after all, the police are going to come searching for the missing animal. If Maddie and I are not really going to run off to Latin America—and with my luck, we wouldn't make it as far as Newark—we're going to have to leave him somewhere. So why not Flamingo Beach? He'll have fresh air, breathtaking views of Manhattan, and an infinite supply of earthworms. What more could an animal with a brain the size of an almond possibly desire? And what better way to destroy the evidence of our impulsive act of larceny? I recognize that Maddie will be dismayed, at first, but I'm optimistic—maybe overly optimistic—that she'll recover eventually. And I can always buy her a replacement: if it works for a mug, why not a turtle? Or, if I should decide to incorporate shell surgery into my show, I'll invest in a pair of the cold-blooded creatures. His-and-hers tortoises. What could be more romantic?

Of course, I won't actually tell Maddie that I liberated Fred. I'll just report that he escaped: one minute, the fellow was sunning himself placidly on the hood of the Buick—and then, an instant later, he managed to vault himself onto a nearby boulder and vanished into the marsh. I will trample down the closest bulrushes as evidence of my efforts to recover him.

I decide to act quickly, before I have the good sense to second-guess myself. I scoop the tortoise off the passenger seat and set him down on a flat patch of granite. He weighs far less than I anticipated, and I resist the urge to fling him into the surf like a discus. "There you go, my boy. Liberty," I declare. "Now make a run for it!"

Fred does not budge. The tortoise thrusts his head out from under his shield and cranes his neck, but immediately recoils. Something in the balmy sea breeze is apparently not to his liking.

"Now's your chance, Freddy. It's a once-in-a-lifetime opportunity," I warn him. "Free at last! Free at last! Thank God Almighty, we are free at last!"

The tortoise's head emerges again, although his legs remain concealed. I take this as a promising sign. "What are you waiting for?" I ask. And in case there's any miscommunication, I settle down on my haunches beside Fred and start to waddle off toward the bed of bog-reeds that fringes the adjoining marsh. "Follow me, my boy. If you don't act now, you're bound to regret it."

No luck. My corduroys are soaked through at the knees, but the dopey tortoise hasn't moved a goddamn inch. My frustration builds: I'm risking a lot for this fellow, and he doesn't have the decency to make an effort. Out on Long Island Sound, a guy sailing a dinghy inspects us through a pair of binoculars; I suppose he's wondering why a person would demonstrate waddling to a tortoise. I flash my middle finger at him. He shrugs and glides away.

I return my attention to Fred and once again shuffle toward the marsh, hoping that he will follow. "Get going," I order. "Before somebody gets angry and runs over you with his car." Fred remains stationary. He has retracted all of his appendages, and the horny scutes of his shell blend easily into the rock face.

I prod him with the toe of my boot. The ingrate should be thankful I don't give him a good solid kick; he'd certainly deserve it. Instead, I do the right thing and scoop him back up in his heavy blanket. Soon enough, he's again settled on the passenger seat, no worse for wear, his dreams of freedom only a distant memory. I flip the air conditioner on mechanically, then shut it off.

"Don't say you didn't have your chance," I say, borrowing his cloth to wipe the perspiration from my neck. "Quite frankly, I'm disappointed in you."

"I have no regrets," replies Fred, now channeling Jimmy Stewart. "All my life I thought I wanted to be free . . . And then freedom was mine for the asking, and I didn't want it any longer. What do I want with liberty when a beautiful massage therapist is willing to feed me earthworms?"

"When you put it that way," I agree.

I hear Maddie before I see her. She opens the

passenger door, her summer dress caked in dirt. "You two boys getting along?"

"We're discussing freedom," I answer. "He's rather a chatty tortoise, once you coax him out of his shell."

"I'm afraid he's also going to be a hungry tortoise," says Maddie. "I couldn't find anything." She returns my mug to the cup holder. It contains a garden snail resting on a fine bed of clipped grass.

"So much for my high-protein dinner."

"We're going to have to take him back," she says. "I don't know what I was thinking before." Maddie polishes the top of the turtle's shell. "Even if we could run off to Mexico, he'd get hurt somehow. I just know it. He'd get sick from the local water, and we wouldn't be able to find a veterinarian. Or we'd leave him in a motel room one afternoon and the maid would prop the door open by mistake. As much as I want to run away, I know it would be selfish." Maddie tickles the belly of Fred's plastron, and he emits a low-pitched gurgle that sounds almost like laughter. "Besides, I completely forgot his kidney pills."

I make a U-turn on the rocks and shift the car into overdrive. We muscle our way up the steep incline toward the main road. As we jounce over stray roots, I worry about the transmission and the tires. Meanwhile, Maddie apologizes to Fred for her shortcomings as a "tortoise mother."

"He almost escaped," I say, "while you were gone."

"I don't want to know," says Maddie. "I'm just glad he didn't."

"Do you think he could have survived out here on

his own?"

"Not in a million years. He'd be breakfast for some lucky hawk or owl before sunrise tomorrow morning." Maggie uses the cloth to remove sand from the folds of Fred's neck. "In any case, he's a desert box turtle. If the humidity out here didn't kill him, the winter certainly would."

"I would have gotten you a new one," I say.

"No you wouldn't have," answers Maddie, her voice cold and sharp. "I wouldn't have spoken to you ever again."

I can tell that she is dead serious, that our relationship has been saved by the intransigence of a stolen tortoise, just as my last two relationships have been undone by my sister's penchant for newborns. The tortoise now appears to be napping, his wrinkled eyelids clamped shut over his bulging eyes. I am also exhausted: far too tired to process the afternoon's escapade. We drive the remainder of the twenty-minute journey to Yonkers in silence. I contemplate telling Maddie about Dr. Whipple, but I will do that later, when I am more awake and I have removed the garden snail from my coffee mug. I now sense that we'll have plenty of time.

Michael has not yet returned home from his roofing job. When he does, he'll have no idea that his tortoise has been briefly kidnapped, just as Maddie will never know how close Fred came to a fatal dose of freedom. I anticipate we will return to this same quiet block next Saturday, and the next, and the one after that, all of us sharing the hostage until something gives.

PARACOSMOS

LESLIE TRACED THEIR DIFFICULTIES to before the parrot-fever scare, to before even the chimney sweep's scrotum, to the summer night when her husband proposed naming the baby Quarantina. "She'll be Tina, for short," said Hugh, who'd recently been appointed public health officer for the county, and only then did Leslie realize he wasn't joking. Other names on his list included Hygienia, Inoculata, and Malaria. "Doesn't Malaria Malansky have a ring to it?" he asked. "She'd be a constant reminder of the work that's yet to be done in the Third World." Leslie preferred Victoria or Elizabeth. In the end, they settled on Eve—after Madame Curie's daughter—but not before the man who was supposed to understand her completely had referred to their future child as a "missed opportunity." So she shouldn't have been terribly shocked, nine years later, when Hugh's intransigence made Evie the pariah of Mrs. Driscoll's fourth-grade classroom.

Evie's best friend that autumn was a chatty, shameless redhead named Kim Pitchford who lived two doors away, and hardly an afternoon passed without that relentless tyke jabbering up a typhoon in their living room. But at lunch one overcast Sunday, Kim informed Evie—and Hugh—that carrying an umbrella increased the likelihood of rain. This roused the scientific lion in Leslie's husband. Hugh delivered an extemporaneous sermon on cause and effect, which began with the unfortunate remark, "Take the scrotum of the chimney sweep," and led to a tale of how some long-dead English surgeon had deduced the relationship between soot and genital tumors. Leslie returned from her tennis match to hear Evie asking, "Papa, what's a chimney sweep?" Three hours later, Rebecca Pitchford phoned to demand an explanation.

"You have to apologize and promise her it won't happen again," Leslie warned her husband. "What were you thinking? Were you thinking?"

"I'm not going to censor myself for some airhead," snapped Hugh. "Men have scrotums. Men die of cancer. That's reality—and nine years old is more than old enough for some basic reality. If I'm going to call Rebecca about anything, it's about all that standing water on their property. To mosquitoes carrying West Nile virus, each of those birdbaths looks like a five-course meal."

And so the conflict with Kim's parents spiraled out

of control. Rebecca Pitchford wouldn't be squaring the circle anytime soon—there was no arguing with Hugh about that—but she did have a vengeful streak, and two weeks later, Evie was the only fourth grader in Hager Hills not invited to Kim's tenth birthday party. In fact, the redhead not only dropped Evie cold but also carried off their daughter's other friends, until one afternoon Leslie's beauty came off the school bus sobbing, "Nobody loves me anymore."

"I love you," cried Leslie, hugging the child to her chest. "Papa loves you." And to console the girl, she promised the only gift Evie wanted even more than the companionship of her peers: a talking parakeet.

Ever since they'd visited the aviary at the Bronx Zoo, Evie had been pleading for a conversational bird. The girl could draw colorful mynahs and cockatiels as though conjured from her imagination, then label each species with precision. She knew both English and Latin names from memory. Even Leslie's personal distaste for birds—their odor, their racket—proved no match for the tears of her rejected child.

"I hope you're not going to be upset," she implored Hugh in bed that night. "It was killing me, seeing her like that. So I agreed we'd get her a parakeet."

"Not in ten million years," said Hugh. "Are you insane?"

"I know it's going to be a hassle—"

"A hassle? It's a hazard. Jesus, Leslie. We're in the middle of a silent psittacosis epidemic." Hugh's eyes locked on hers. "Parrot fever. Ornithosis. Two years ago, a pet-shop owner died right down the turnpike in New Brunswick. Do you really want to expose Evie to pneumonia—to meningitis?"

"But plenty of people own parakeets," pleaded Leslie.

"Plenty of people also smoke cigarettes and eat raw shellfish and ride motorcycles without helmets. Evie isn't plenty of people." Hugh caressed her bare shoulder. "Look, I'm sorry. If I'd known Rebecca was such a bitch, I'd have swallowed my pride."

"You still could . . ."

"I already phoned her from the office. She wasn't interested."

So the next evening, they sat down together with Evie in her intensely pink bedroom and explained why she couldn't have a parakeet. To Leslie's surprise, their daughter merely shrugged off the disappointment. "Lauren brought her macaw over for our sleepover," said Evie. "And her macaw knows five thousand words."

Leslie exchanged a nervous glance with her husband. "Lauren?" she asked.

"My new best friend," said Evie. Then she turned to a patch of vacant air, between the halogen floor lamp and the colossal stuffed leopard her uncle had won for her at a carnival, and she ordered Lauren, "Tell your macaw to say something."

After a splash of silence, Evie bubbled with laughter.

"See," said their daughter between giggles. "Isn't she great?"

Leslie looked to Hugh for guidance, but he was staring

at the empty space, wearing an expression of bewilderment. With each passing second of laughter, she felt Evie drifting further from her toward a world of imaginary birds.

"What did Lauren's macaw say, princess?" she finally asked.

Her daughter's laughter faded into a sullen pout.

"Come on, Mommy. Listen carefully."

In the foyer ten minutes later, Leslie found her entire body trembling. "I'm scared, Hugh. She's too old for imaginary friends."

"It's a phase. It's perfectly healthy," Hugh reassured her. "Let's just hope that Lauren's mother is less of a bitch than Kim's."

&

Sally Whiskers had been Leslie's invisible companion for a brief spell during her own childhood: a chimeric creature, part-human and part-feline, who fulfilled Leslie's desires for both a best friend and a house cat. They'd hunted mice together in kindergarten—much to the alarm of the school psychologist. But in first grade, her twin brother asserted that he was also friends with Sally, and Leslie still remembered the car ride when she contended he was lying, that he couldn't be friends with Sally, because Sally didn't exist. And that had been that. Hugh, she was amused and delighted to discover, also once befriended a daydream. Doctor Charley Horse. Her husband had even demanded that his father buy the make-believe physician a plastic stethoscope of his own.

But if Evie had inherited a proclivity for fantasy from both of her parents, Leslie sensed at the outset that Lauren Dowdy was different: more complex, more demanding, more real.

While chatty Kim Pitchford had been a daily visitor to their home, voiceless Lauren practically moved in. She joined them for supper every evening, and Evie insisted that a place setting be laid out for her at the kitchen table. Some mornings, the child slept over and stayed for breakfast—and Evie insisted on filling a second bowl of cereal, then discarding it when Lauren didn't eat on account of a "tummy ache." The imaginary girl required her own toothbrush, her own jack-o'-lantern at Halloween, her own turn when her grandfather bestowed piggyback rides. Leslie's brother took Evie and his three daughters to the grand opening of Adventure America—an indoor amusement park in Atlantic City—and he had to negotiate a separate seat for the invisible girl on the carousel. Evie's new playmate boasted a rich and uncannily consistent history that set her apart from the run-of-the-mill pretend friends that Leslie read about on the Internet. She had a birthday, a scar on her right knee from a water-skiing mishap, even a nickel allergy. Like Kim, she boasted fiery red hair and chalk-pale skin. On a whim, Leslie asked if Lauren Dowdy had any siblings. "An older sister, but she drowned," Evie answered with a precision that unsettled her mother. "And her parents are divorced, so she can't have any more." One day, the macaw taught Lauren and Evie an obscene word for oral intercourse.

At first, Leslie believed Lauren to be a stand-in for her daughter's disloyal friends—that all it required to banish the imaginary girl back into stardust would be a renewal of Evie's former relationships or overtures from other potential playmates. But when a happy-go-lucky eleven-year-old brunette named Melissa moved into the bungalow across the street and invited Evie to go bowling with her family, Leslie's daughter adamantly refused—because she'd promised Lauren that they'd spend the day together expanding her macaw's vocabulary. Even a phone call from Kim Pitchford went unanswered. "Tell her I'm playing with Lauren," commanded Evie with uncharacteristic ferocity. "Lauren is my best friend now. I don't need two best friends." The next week was Evie's own birthday, but she warned Leslie in advance not to purchase her a Queen Anne dollhouse, even though she'd been begging for that particular gift all year. "I don't want to make Lauren jealous," she explained after the other girl had supposedly walked home. "If you buy me a dollhouse, you have to buy her one, too. Okay?" Had Evie been somebody else's daughter, this appeal would have seemed touching, even humorous.

Hugh urged her to take Evie's behavior in stride—if you normalize it, she'll grow out of it sooner—but following the dollhouse plea, Leslie suspected that this was far more than a mere phase, that her daughter's long-term mental health might be seriously endangered. That night, she waited until Hugh had powered down his laptop and was about to turn off the bedside lamp. (Although she hated confrontation—even preferred her own suffering to an argument—she could stomach an argument for her daughter's sake.) "We need to do something about Evie," she announced. "I know you're convinced this will pass. But it's been three months already, and it's not passing."

Her husband released the lamp switch with reluctance, obviously unenthusiastic about discussing their daughter's psyche. What had initially attracted Leslie to Hugh—his zeal for scientific rationality, his stoicism in the face of crisis—proved exasperating in matters of child rearing.

"It's not causing her any distress," he said. "Why get worked up?"

"It's causing me distress," answered Leslie. "I want to take her to a doctor."

Hugh shook his head, grinning. "I am a doctor," he said—as she had anticipated he would.

"You're an epidemiologist." They'd had this same conversation before, every time she'd suggested phoning their pediatrician over a rash or a fever. "I mean a real doctor. Maybe even a psychiatrist."

Giving voice to the word "psychiatrist" somehow made her daughter's condition more critical, like the word "terminal" had once made her mother's lung fibrosis.

"In the first place, four years of medical school says I'm very much a real doctor, Mrs. Malansky, thank you very much," retorted her husband. "Probably more real than any half-witted headshrinker. And in the second place, I don't think we're there yet. If you're genuinely concerned, we'll sit down with Evie and figure out what she's really thinking. For all you know, she could admit that this Lauren girl is entirely imaginary."

That was Hugh: always a plan, always in control.

The next evening, at bedtime, they accompanied Evie into her room for a "heart-to-heart-to-heart." Leslie sat at the foot of the bed, letting the child rest her pajama-clad legs across her lap. Hugh settled backward onto an undersized desk chair. He'd been inspecting agricultural sites all afternoon, and he still had a badge reading "VISITOR – SESTITO'S DAIRY" stuck to his shirt breast. Leslie waited for him to broach the perilous matter of Lauren. Instead, Evie asked, "Am I in trouble?"

"No, you're not in trouble, princess," Leslie soothed. "Hugh, tell her we're not upset with her."

"Of course, we're not upset with you," began Hugh, palms resting on his folded knee, leaning forward like a country physician, his glasses perched halfway down the bridge of his sharp nose. "We're just concerned. I know you were upset about the parakeet . . . and about that Pitchford girl."

"Oh, Papa. You're so silly. There's nothing to be worried about," interjected Evie. The girl lay surrounded by plush animals and frilled throw pillows. "Now that Lauren and I are best friends forever, I don't care about Kim. Not at all. Anyway, Kim was a bitch."

Leslie winced. Hugh ignored the profanity. "Your mother and I want to make sure you realize Lauren is imaginary." Even as her husband spoke, Leslie felt like a monster—as though they had denied the existence of Santa Claus or the tooth fairy.

Evie folded her slender arms across her chest. "She is not imaginary. She's standing right there." She pointed to empty air. "That was mean, Papa. Now you've upset her."

"She is imaginary," replied Hugh, keeping his tone level and matter-of-fact. "You're a big girl, Evie, and it's important that you recognize the difference between real things and imaginary things."

"Lauren is not a thing. She's a person," Evie shot back. "Please stop talking about her before you hurt her feelings even more. It's past my bedtime."

Hugh stood up and strode to the door, conveying an air of decision. "You're welcome to play make-believe all you wish, honey. But from this moment forward, your mother and I are going to treat you like an adult." Reluctantly, after embracing her daughter, Leslie followed him out of the room.

"Now what?" she asked.

"We do exactly what I said," he replied. "She can keep playing with that imaginary girlfriend all she wishes. But that doesn't mean we have to."

Leslie did her utmost—the whole day Saturday—to comply with her husband's instructions. When Evie boasted that Lauren had received the highest score on Mrs. Driscoll's spelling quiz the previous week, she nodded noncommittally. And fearing that Evie would demand two identical bowls of ice cream after lunch, she instructed her daughter to serve the dessert herself. That way Evie, not she, was responsible for the mint-chocolate-flavored soup she later discarded down the drain. But this impasse could only endure so long, and it finally broke at dinner.

Hugh had been summoned to West Asbury shortly

after dawn to investigate an outbreak of food poisoning; he returned home exhausted and cranky following an argument with the owner of a sushi bar who'd refused to surrender the names of his suppliers. Leslie hoped to cheer up her husband by baking one of his favorite meals, salmon in garlic butter. She let Evie do the serving, dodging responsibility for the piece of sizzling fish that went untouched at the fourth place setting. At first, Hugh said nothing. But when he finished his own portion, he scooped the salmon off the extra plate and onto his own.

"Put that back," commanded Evie. "It's Lauren's."

"No, it's not," answered Hugh. "Because Lauren doesn't exist."

A look of anguish colored Evie's features. And then, without warning, she threw her fork across the room into the refrigerator door. The implement clattered to the ground, dislodging several magnets in the process.

Hugh grabbed his daughter's wrist. The girl burst into sobs.

"Please, Hugh," cried Leslie. "You're hurting her."

"I am not hurting her," he said. "But we're done with imaginary girlfriends. You can do whatever you wish when you're off on your own, young lady, but when you're inside this house, we'll have no more talk of Lauren—or any other make-believe."

"Let go of her," pleaded Leslie.

Hugh relinquished his grip. "I swear, if you pretend to invite that girl home with you again, I'll pretend to spank the living daylights out of her until she can't sit down for weeks. Am I making myself clear?"

Evie said nothing. She hugged her arms around her torso, and her lower lip quivered. When Leslie tried to embrace her, she ran to her bedroom and buried her head under the covers.

Leslie's daughter did not mention Lauren again. For several days, she roamed the house sullenly, speaking only when spoken to, but increasingly she requested permission to play with Melissa and other girls in the neighborhood. Hugh saw this as evidence that his daughter was perfectly healthy. But Leslie, who'd grown accustomed to having two nine-year-old girls in her home at all hours of the day—first two real ones, then one real and one imaginary—now found the gray silence of the late afternoons disheartening. For the first time ever, she second-guessed leaving her job at the library to play full-time mom. She even considered returning to school for graduate work, possibly acquiring a degree in public health so she could better understand the papers Hugh published in journals like The Bulletin of Waterborne Illnesses. Four afternoons straight, she sat at the bay windows in the living room, reading a novel and periodically peering between the blinds in the hope that Evie might bring one of her friends—real or imagined—home for a playdate. Instead, the girls exited the bus and retreated through Melissa's front door.

On the fourth afternoon, as Leslie gazed at the spot

where, moments earlier, her daughter had disembarked, a weather-beaten Oldsmobile sedan pulled up to the curbside. It was the species of automobile that Hugh always cursed for its poor gas mileage and environmental impact. "You might as well pump lead into the atmosphere," her husband complained. From the vehicle emerged a broad-shouldered man in his forties, unmistakably handsome despite a noticeable gut. He drew a final drag from his cigarette, crushed it under his boot, then strolled up the Malanskys' flagstone walk with his hands in his pockets. Leslie answered the doorbell with a sense of foreboding, as a military mother might greet an unfamiliar officer.

"Mrs. Malansky?" asked the visitor.

She smiled, still clutching the doorknob.

"Steve Dowdy," he introduced himself. "I was hoping you might have a moment to talk about your daughter. Is this a good time?"

At first, she feared he might be an emissary from the school district: A psychologist? A social worker? A truant officer? Yet his last name was familiar. Her stomach muscles tightened. "Is something wrong with Evie?"

"That's what I've come to find out," he replied. "I'm her friend Lauren's father. Or her ex-friend, it now seems. May I come in?"

Later, Leslie couldn't recall inviting Steve Dowdy inside, but somehow she found herself sitting opposite him in the living room. It crossed her mind that she might be the victim of some sick joke, but neither Hugh nor her brother had an appetite for pranks, and nobody else, other than Evie herself, was aware of the imaginary child's banishment. Listening as her guest revealed his concerns—in a voice both tender and firm—Leslie knew deep down that this man was not part of any prank.

"Lauren's totally heartbroken," Steve Dowdy explained. "She spends most weeknights with her mother, so it wasn't until yesterday that I realized how upset she is." Leslie's eyes dropped toward his strong hands. "You probably think it's crazy of me to come here like this. My ex told me to mind my own business," he added. "Getting rejected is part of a normal childhood, she said. But Lauren means everything to me, Leslie, and it tears my heart up to see her suffering . . . So I guess I was hoping you might be willing to put in a good word for her with Evie." He looked up at her hopefully, and his self-assurance had melted into an adorable sheepishness.

Never in her life had another adult touched Leslie so deeply. She couldn't conceive of Hugh pleading Evie's case to some other girl's parents, if the circumstances had been reversed—certainly not with such humility.

"I'm so sorry," said Leslie. "To be candid, this is my husband's doing. He's a scientist. He doesn't like . . ." She was going to say "make-believe," but she suddenly realized how absurd that sounded. Steve Dowdy obviously didn't think his daughter was imaginary—and she couldn't be imaginary if her father was a flesh-and-blood human being sitting on the sofa, could she? She'd figure out the mystery later, she decided. For now, her goal was to appease her guest. "Hugh has certain prejudices," she tried again. "He was worried that our girls had become too dependent on each other, that Evie wasn't making other friends. And once my husband gets an idea into his skull, you'd have to saw his head off to remove it. I'm afraid he won't tolerate your daughter in our house, at present. But I don't see why the girls can't play together at school." Leslie hadn't intended to run down her husband; she found her gaze locked on Dowdy's, and she looked away quickly. "I'll certainly say something to Evie, I promise."

Steve Dowdy beamed. "That would be wonderful," he said. "I was afraid you might think I was ridiculous."

"I think you're lovely," blurted Leslie.

A hush fell over the living room, pierced only by the distant murmur of the heating system. Leslie toyed with her wedding ring, her eyes focused across the carpet, on the front leg of the piano bench. She sensed heat suffusing her cheeks.

"Lauren was right about you," said Steve Dowdy.

She turned to him in curiosity, also apprehension.

"You are beautiful," he elaborated. "More beautiful than I thought possible."

And then he kissed her: the father of her daughter's imaginary ex-best friend, a man who shouldn't exist but whose lips felt far more real than anything she'd experienced in many years. He kissed her, and he kissed her, and then they stumbled to her bedroom. The room was snug, dark, illuminated only through one partially drawn curtain. Even while she was enveloped in Steve Dowdy's arms, Leslie felt outside of herself, watching her own body, dazed by her affection for this alien being. And yet she was happy, maybe happier than she'd been since before Evie's birth.

Afterward, he sang for her what had once been Lauren's favorite lullaby, a heartwarming tale about a lonely kangaroo who befriends a koala bear.

"Would you mind if I smoked?" he asked.

Under ordinary circumstances, she'd rather have let him sprinkle uranium isotopes inside her refrigerator. But these were not ordinary circumstances.

"I guess not," she said.

"Thanks." He plucked his jeans from the carpet and retrieved his lighter. "I have nothing against public health in principle," he explained. "But in practice, all the longevity in the world doesn't taste as good as a thick, juicy steak."

Steve Dowdy's cigarette filled the room with the cozy scent of tobacco, a transgression somehow even more sinful than extramarital sex. You're incorrigible today, Leslie said to herself—but with surprise and bemusement, not guilt. She barely managed to air out the house before Hugh returned home from the office.

Guilt arrived soon enough. Steve Dowdy appeared at the same hour the next afternoon, but said nothing of his daughter—and while they were making love, in the double bed that smelled faintly of Hugh's aftershave and socks—Leslie found herself thinking: I'm having an affair. Me! The stark tangibility of this fact amazed her. She had known other women over the years who'd confided to her that they'd cheated on their husbands—a garrulous aide in the library's reference room, a former Vassar classmate who'd seduced an electrician—but Leslie felt genuinely baffled to be among these women. The improbability of her role knocked her so far off guard that, during the ensuing week, she nearly forgot that her lover's daughter was supposedly imaginary. In fact, she strove not to think about this enigma. When their conversation drifted to matters that might prove his claims fraudulent, or metaphysically impossible, she steered them back toward the profoundly mundane.

It was inevitable, of course, that Steve Dowdy's outside life would come up during their long talks about love and parenting, and Leslie noted that his stories dovetailed perfectly with what she'd previously learned from Evie. Her lover was a Peace Corps veteran, a part-time psychology professor with a modest private practice. (She even discovered his name and credentials, but not his photograph, on the faculty website for Hager County Community College.) His ex-wife had divorced him for a dental hygienist who'd once been Miss Teen Venezuela and who'd subsequently run off with her manicurist. On the first day Leslie and Steve left the house together—for coffee at the local diner, while Evie attended her weekly violin lesson—her lover described how he'd discovered the body of Lauren's older sister, Amanda, at the bottom of his neighbor's pool. "Patti thought she was with me, and I thought she was with Patti . . . and somehow she climbed through this little gap in their fence," he said. "It was a tiny hole. Tiny! You wouldn't have believed a

rabbit could squeeze through, let alone a four-year-old."
Leslie instinctively clasped his hand, even though they were
in a public restaurant, not caring who might see her.

Fortunately, Hugh's public health efforts kept him on
the job later than usual that month. On the same afternoon
that Steve entered Leslie's life, her husband labored overtime
probing a tuberculosis cluster at a chemical plant. Two days
later, he phoned to warn Leslie he'd be home well after dark,
as he'd been asked by the mayors of several coastal hamlets
to learn whether a colony of low-flying bats carried rabies.
Hugh's workaholic fervor, which had so often frustrated
Leslie in the past, now afforded her extra time to prepare
his dinners. On occasion, she even suspected he might be
faking his responsibilities—that Hugh somehow sensed she
was having an affair and, wanting to avoid confrontation,
gave her a wide berth. Of course, Hugh wasn't a man to
avoid confrontation. In fact, he thrived on it. So, more
likely, he was too absorbed in his own work to notice her
distance. In any case, the only time he voiced concerns was
that first night, when he inquired whether anyone had been
smoking inside the house. "Did you go someplace smoky?"
he pressed. "The smell must be clinging to your clothes."
After that, she exiled Steve's cancer sticks to the back patio.

Although Leslie had promised Dowdy that she'd put
in a good word for his daughter with Evie, two weeks elapsed
before she finally mustered the courage. She truly did want
to help Lauren—if the girl even existed—but she feared
unsettling her own child, who appeared to have embraced
the carefree, somewhat dopey Melissa as her latest ideal

playmate. Leslie finally introduced the subject on a chilly Sunday in November, en route to purchase her daughter a new pair of mittens. "Do you ever play with Lauren Dowdy anymore?" she asked, apropos of absolutely nothing.

Evie eyed her suspiciously. "No. You told me not to."

"I know we did," conceded Leslie. "I think your father and I were afraid you were going overboard—preferring her to your other friends. But if you wanted to hang out with her once in a while, especially at school, that would be fine."

She dared not refer to the girl as either real or imaginary. Instead, Steve Dowdy's daughter occupied a narrow passage between truth and fiction.

"Lauren has new friends," replied Evie. "And Melissa is my best friend now."

How intense and fluid relationships were at that age!

But she had done her part. She had tried.

What Leslie did not do, on the days she ran into Melissa Steinhoff's mother in the organic market or crossed paths with Rebecca Pitchford at the municipal tennis pavilion, was ask whether they knew about a girl named Lauren Dowdy. Because she was afraid of their answers. Because whether Steve was the product of a coincidence or a hoax or a paranormal vortex, she did not want to lose him. She treasured the way her lover asked after every detail of Evie's life—even though she never made similar inquiries about Lauren—so that he probably knew more about her child's daily existence than did her own husband. Besides, Leslie assured herself in a moment of levity, how could their romance be wrong if Steve didn't even exist?

And yet it did feel wrong! She'd been brought up in a traditional home, two parents, one brother, zero imaginary lovers. Duplicity did not come naturally to her, although—for the record—she hadn't actively lied to Hugh about anything beyond that initial cigarette. She hadn't needed to. Instead, her falsehoods were falsehoods of omission, deceptions that festered beneath the pelt of her marriage. She sensed herself in limbo, tugged in both directions, although nobody was actually doing any tugging. She kept waiting for Steve to demand more of her—even to insist that she abandon her marriage. He didn't. He merely brought her daffodils, and biographies of Carl Jung, and perfect afternoons of seemingly inexhaustible passion. Ultimately, it was Leslie who sought to impose a trajectory on their relationship.

They took advantage of the fourth grade's class field trip to the maritime museum in Seacroft and decided to risk a late lunch at a romantic bistro opposite the Hager Hills harbor. Hugh had been grabbing meals at the office all week, so she didn't even have to worry about his supper. It was a crisp November afternoon—nearly Thanksgiving—and on the stroll across the vacant parking lot, Leslie warmed her hand in Steve's coat pocket. Inside, they opted for a table far from the windows, claiming that they feared the draft. Their waitress lit a candle in a glass jar and handed them each a menu, then sashayed into the kitchen. The only other patron was an elderly, bow-tied gentleman seated at the bar, playing solitaire. He glanced their way for a moment, then returned to his cards.

"So," said Leslie. "That old man probably thinks

we're married."

Steve glanced across the restaurant. "One of us is married."

His remark struck her as flippant. "You don't have to remind me," Leslie replied. She took a deep breath, studied the thick veins on the backs of his hands. "Look," she said, "I don't want to ruin things, but I hate running around in secret like this."

Steve nodded. "All right. What do you want?"

The problem was that she genuinely didn't know. She didn't want to be having an affair, and she didn't want to leave Hugh, and she certainly didn't want to end her relationship with Steve, but those three sentiments were obviously incompatible. The enigma of her lover's daughter, still impenetrable, added to her uncertainty. But you couldn't exactly tell a man you'd been sleeping with for four weeks that you weren't sure whether his daughter was real or imaginary.

"I guess I want to know where we're headed," she finally said.

Her lover traced his fingers along the edge of his menu. His face looked weary in the candlelight. "Do we have to be headed somewhere? Can't we just be?"

His wish sounded so reasonable—yet so infuriating.

"What do I want?" she asked aloud, as though no time had elapsed since his earlier question. "I suppose I want to be a larger part of your life. Sometimes, I feel like I don't know you. We've been getting together like this for a whole month, and I haven't even met your daughter."

Steve's expression turned from worn to wary. "I don't understand. Patti told me Lauren practically spent the entire summer at your house."

This was her moment to demand an explanation, but she lacked the nerve. Blood pounded in her temples. "She wasn't around that often," Leslie lied, struggling to recover. She forced a smile. "Hugh used to take the girls with him on his investigations and then drop Lauren off at her mother's on the way home."

No sooner had the words left her tongue than she realized how inappropriate it would have been for her husband to expose another man's child to outbreaks of salmonella and swine flu. Luckily, Steve didn't protest. He still appeared to be digesting her admission about not knowing his daughter.

"I would like to meet her," said Leslie. "Very much . . . Can I?"

Her lover's expression turned hesitant. "I guess," he replied.

"When?"

"I don't know, really. Soon."

"How about tomorrow?" pushed Leslie.

Steve shook his head. "Soon," he said again. "Patti and I have a custody agreement. It's complicated. Not something that we can figure out overnight."

Something in his demeanor told Leslie that what prevented her from meeting his daughter was more than logistics. She didn't raise the matter again during their meal. Instead they discussed her own father's new "lady friend," the upcoming PBS documentary about Sigmund Freud, and Evie's progress on the violin—all topics that, at this particular moment, interested neither of them. In the parking lot, she returned to the subject she'd been thinking about through the meal.

"I really do want to meet your daughter," she said. "Can we set a date? Maybe something a few weeks from now?"

Her companion stopped walking, and his entire body appeared to tense up. "I told you, soon. Why isn't that sufficient?"

She'd never seen him grow irritated before. Rather than causing her to back off—as she might have done with her husband, or almost anyone else—Steve's attitude provoked her.

"I want to name a date," she answered. "A commitment."

Leslie was now fully aware of how unreasonable, even petulant, she sounded.

"I can't give you a date," Steve snapped. Then he paused, and apologized. "I didn't mean to jump on you," he said. "I'm sorry. It's just that Patti has a job offer in another state, and everything's up in the air at the moment. She wants to relocate, and she wants to take Lauren with her—and our custody arrangement lets her do that."

"You'd move, too?"

Steve gazed into the distance, across the concrete plaza to the masts poking up at the marina. Overhead, gulls circled. "I don't know," he said. "I have a job here, a practice . . . and other things." He looked at her, and she knew that she was what he meant by other things, but his face had lost some of its tenderness.

When her lover failed to appear on her front porch the next afternoon at three o'clock, as he always had, Leslie chose not to phone the number that he'd given her for emergencies—chose not to learn what she might discover at the other end of the line. Even as the winter sun dipped behind the roof of the Steinhoffs' bungalow, she understood that she'd never see Steve Dowdy again.

That night, Hugh returned home from the office earlier than usual—his mood sullen and grim. At dinner, he hardly touched his halibut. "Haven't I asked you not to buy fish with high mercury content?" he demanded. "Do you want to turn your daughter into the Mad Hatter?"

"I checked the danger list," objected Leslie. "Halibut's not on it."

Hugh frowned. "Well, it should be."

She saw that something must have happened at the health department, but she wasn't in any frame of mind to discuss it; all she'd been able to think about for the past four hours was Steve Dowdy. And although she'd seen him only a day earlier, their entire relationship now seemed a cruel trick of her own imagination. Someday, she might ask Evie about the girl, she understood, or even make inquiries of Rebecca Pitchford and Phyllis Steinhoff—but not yet. Besides, she feared she already knew what she'd learn.

To her amazement, Hugh suddenly inquired after

the child.

"Evie," he asked, "do you ever run into that Lauren Dowdy girl?"

Evie offered him a blank expression. "Who?"

"The friend—the make-believe friend—you used to play with. The one who had the invisible parrot."

Leslie's daughter stared at her father. "Don't be silly, Papa. There's no such thing as an invisible parrot."

"Obviously, there isn't," agreed Hugh. "But just the same, do you ever . . . imagine running into Lauren?"

Evie returned to her food. "I don't know what you're talking about, Papa. I've never had any friend named Lauren. Are you sure you don't mean Kim?"

"No," answered Hugh. "I'm not sure."

They ate the remainder of the meal in relative silence—each of them lost in private thoughts. At first, Evie posed her standard repertoire of questions: How old do seals live to be? What's the difference between turquoise and blue-green? But eventually she took the hint from Leslie's terse answers that nobody wanted to talk.

And yet, the moment that Evie excused herself from the dinner table, they both immediately returned to the subject of Lauren.

"She doesn't remember—"

"Probably blocked it out."

Hugh laughed unexpectedly.

"What's so funny?" Leslie asked.

"I was just thinking how glad I am that Lauren's mother turned out to be less of a bitch than Kim's."

That sent a bolt of rage cascading through Leslie's soul. "What is that supposed to mean? How the hell do you know Lauren's mother?"

Hugh grimaced. "That was a joke, Leslie. A joke." He abruptly stood up and began clearing their plates. "For Christ's sake, you sound like you're jealous. Which part of make-believe don't you understand?"

"Sure," agreed Leslie. "A joke. Ha, ha."

But the more Leslie reflected on Lauren Dowdy's mother, and whether she'd had a relationship with Hugh, the less of a joke it seemed. It certainly didn't seem like a joke two weeks later, when she took Evie and moved into an efficiency apartment near the waterfront, or the following month, when her attorney served the divorce papers. What it had been—if not a joke—Leslie could never say. And when she finally did buy her daughter a scarlet macaw, the following summer, she was not surprised that Evie insisted on naming the bird Lauren. Far better than Quarantina or Malaria, Leslie thought. Far more real.

CPSIA information can be obtained at www.ICGtesting.com
Printed in the USA
BVOW08s0531070515

399214BV00002B/42/P

9 780984 940585